I0663818

The Vengeance Squad Goes To Germany

Sidney W. Frost

Published by Sidney W. Frost
153 Cattle Trail Way
Georgetown, TX 78633
sidfrost@suddenlink.net
http://sidneywfrost.com

Printed in the United States by CreateSpace.com

Editor: Lisa Lickel
Proofreaders: D.A. Featherling and Malia Barth

Couple Photo: © Rshkri | Dreamstime.com—Fence With Barbed Wire Photo

ISBN: 0-9903181-4-1
ISBN-13: 978-0-9903181-4-9

DEDICATION

In this book, the antagonists
pretend to be refugees and,
in doing so, make all refugees
appear evil. That is not my intent.
There are millions of refugees
with strong moral character
who work hard to find a
haven for their loved ones.
This book is dedicated to them.

CHAPTER ONE

Angela McCowan's left cheek touched a tacky floor in a dark room. The odor of stale beer and rotted food clogged her nostrils.

She pushed to stand, the floor's stickiness coated both her palms. It didn't matter. Pain throbbed from the top of her head to her legs. She fell back to the floor to catch her breath.

She turned over. Looked up. Moonlight filtered in through small windows, too high to reach. Her eyes adjusted to the gray shadows that surrounded her. Was she alone?

Stand. Run. Escape.

She had been near the immigrant refugee camp. The new one in Berlin, Germany. Where the old airport used to be. She was on foot, thinking about home on her way to meet her partner when a black van screeched to a stop beside her. Two men grabbed her from behind and tossed her into the back of the vehicle. One climbed in and jammed a gun in her ribs.

It was over quickly. Had Nathan seen what had happened? Was he okay? Was he searching for her?

Someone had held a wet cloth to her face . . . the smell of chloroform . . .

Memory stopped.

She'd been kidnapped.

Did abductors know who she was, who she worked for?

In the near darkness, on her back, she felt her body for other pains, lingering a little longer on her abdomen where a new pain worried her. She thanked God she wasn't hurt.

It took all her strength to get to her feet, but she had to find a way out. She hadn't gone but a few feet when a mound big enough to be a body caught her attention. She reached for her weapon . . . only to find it wasn't there.

***

Tex was home when his phone rang. It was time for a day off from his Austin-based clientele, something he tried to do at least once a month to study the latest journals on substance abuse counseling.

He didn't usually take phone calls on study days, but he checked the caller ID to make sure it wasn't Jane. He smiled when Doc's name popped up. His friend lived in England, but they managed to talk at least once a month.

"Howdy, Doc." Tex was the only one in their group of friends who called Chris "Doc". Chris was still Christopher J. McCowan, PhD, former computer professor, to him. Out of friendship, he shortened it to Doc.

He waited, but there was no response. Tex looked at his phone. It appeared to be working. "Hey. You there?"

He put the phone back to his ear and waited. He was about to hang up when the professor's voice answered.

"Tex? Yes. I'm here. Sorry. A call came in right as you answered. I had to deal with it."

"Good to hear from you, man. How're you and your bride doing?"

"I need your help."

Tex still dabbled in computers after his college courses with Doc, and kept up with the latest techniques, but it was merely a hobby for him. Because of the level of difficulty often involved in what Doc was doing, it was an honor to be needed and gave him a reason to maintain his skills. Besides, he enjoyed talking about the latest computer-hacking techniques. Usually, all Doc needed was someone to listen, something Tex did well.

"Okay. Tell me about it."

"I'll tell you when you get here." Doc's voice was flat, hardly recognizable.

"Huh? What do you mean *get here*?"

"I need you. Talk to Liz. Coordinate your travel plans with her."

"Liz is going to England?"

"I haven't talked to her yet, but I'm sure she will."

Tex didn't know what to say. "Uh ... Give me *something*. If you want me to go all that way, I'll have to convince Jane. What do I tell her?"

"She'll understand."

The phone went dead.

He stared at the screen. Should he call back? Doc expected him to drop everything and go to England. For what?

He slipped the phone into his breast pocket and rolled his wheelchair to the kitchen. Looking around in a momentary fog, he finally reached for a cup and filled it with coffee.

The kitchen door opened and his wife walked in both hands grasping plastic grocery bags.

She smiled. "Hi, honey. Enjoying your day off?"

"I was." He paused. "Until Doc called."

"Chris called? How are he and Angela?" She put the grocery bags on the island in the middle of the kitchen and stood in front of his wheelchair giving him her full attention.

Tex reached out for her hands. "It was the strangest thing I've ever heard. Something is wrong, but he didn't tell me what."

"What *did* he say?"

"He wants me to go there."

"To England?"

"Yes. He said it was important and he wants me

4

there as soon as possible."

Jane pulled away from Tex's grip and reached for a cup. "Is this stuff fresh?"

"Uh . . . kind of." He looked at his watch.

She smelled the dark brew, poured half a cup, and added a little hot water.

He followed her with his eyes. "Weird, right? He wants me to put my life and career on hold and drop everything to go help him with something. Some problem he can't discuss on the phone."

Jane frowned. "Did he mention Angela?"

"No." He'd meant to ask about Doc's wife, but the call ended so abruptly there wasn't time.

"That's strange."

Tex considered that. "Doc said *he* needed help, not *they* needed help."

"What about Liz? Did he mention her?"

"Funny you asked. He said he hadn't talked to her yet, but to coordinate travel plans with her. Like he's sure she's gonna do it."

She nodded. "I thought he might have called her."

Jane walked around the island and started to unload the grocery bags. "Okay, you have to go."

Tex wheeled around to face her. That was the last thing he expected. "I do? Why?"

"Think about it. Don't you see what's happening? He's activating the Vengeance Squad and he's doing it for a reason so serious he can't say the words out loud. He needs you. And knowing Chris, and his record of independence, he wouldn't have called unless it was his last resort."

"Hmm. You're right. But he could have said *why* he needs us. That would give us time to prepare. Time to consider how his request will impact our lives. After my accident, I thought I'd end up on the streets again. If you hadn't been there and helped me through the dark times, I wouldn't be where I am now. I'm afraid of jeopardizing all I've accomplished by running off somewhere playing detective with the Vengeance Squad."

Jane knelt before him and looked into his eyes. "It wasn't me alone who helped you. Chris and Liz did, too. She gave you a job at the city library when no one else would. And she helped get your student loans paid off. Chris was always there for you. He'd do anything for you. Besides, none of that matters. He wouldn't have called if it wasn't important."

She went back to putting away the groceries. "I suspect his problem has something to do with Angela. She must be in trouble."

"She's *always* in trouble. She's an MI6 agent for goodness' sakes."

"Yeah, but usually she can handle it. Have you called Liz?"

"No. But . . . are you sure? I hate having to leave everything to you. You have your work and the kids."

"I can manage. Your parents will help. They're always looking for an excuse to spend more time with their grandkids. You have to go."

"But, but . . . "

"But, nothing. What would he do if you needed him?"

Tex hung his head and didn't answer. There was no need to. They both knew Doc would be on the next plane to the States if Tex needed him.

A sense of anticipation tingled along his spine. He couldn't help but wonder. What adventures would they share this time?

***

Michael stepped out of the Texas late winter sun and into the Georgetown bookmobile. He handed his phone to his grandmother, Liz Helmsley.

"It's Chris. He wants to talk to you."

Liz took the phone and put it to her ear. Michael had probably told Chris about their little adventure in Sun City, Texas and Chris was going to congratulate her on solving another case, such as it was.

"Hello there," she said with a slight chuckle, anticipating Chris's compliments.

"Liz, I need you to come to England. Right away."

She grabbed a breath. "What's wrong?"

"I can't say anything on the phone except I need you here. Can you come?"

She knew by the sound of his voice it was important. "Certainly. When and where?" She hoped she could live up to her bravado. What would happen to the library service? And Samuel? Michael? Princess? Was she strong enough? She felt fine, but she was getting up there in years. She was at that age when many began to slow down, even though she hoped it never happened to her.

"Meet me in Hemington . . . as soon as you can."

"I need to tell Samuel and Michael how long I'll be gone. Will you tell me that?"

"No." His voice paused. "Only because I don't know. I've already talked to Michael about handling the bookmobile service. He'll be a part of our support team, working from there. Bring Samuel with you. It'll be nice to have someone here at the house while we're gone."

"Where are we going?"

"I'll tell you everything when you get here."

Liz felt herself shaking. Was it excitement or fear? "What about Percy and Jane?" Other than his parents, Liz was the only one who called Tex by his given name.

"I just got off the phone with Tex. I'm sure he's coming. Can't say Jane will, but she's welcome. Coordinate your travel plans with him."

Liz was surprised Percy would leave his clients for long. Plus Percy and Jane had made their children a priority in their lives after their last adventure with the Vengeance Squad in the United Kingdom. If Percy was willing to go help, perhaps he knew more about the plan than Chris had told her.

She tried another question. "You can't say *why* you want us there?"

"It'd be best not to discuss it on the phone."

Liz hesitated. "I want to be there, but let me check with Samuel."

"Of course. Call me in two hours. We need to move on this quickly. And, no matter what you decide,

I'll understand and always treasure your friendship."

The line went dead.

"Michael. Let's shut it down. We're going home."

He went to work preparing the bookmobile for departure.

"Oh, dear . . . oh, dear . . . oh, dear . . . . What is Samuel going to think?"

Michael climbed aboard. "What'd you say?"

"Nothing, dear. Drive us to the farm. I've got to tell Samuel what Chris wants. And I need to pray while you drive."

Michael looked at her as if waiting for an explanation. When none came, he seated himself behind the steering wheel and started the engine.

CHAPTER TWO

Angela's eyes adjusted to her surroundings. The bulge on the floor was shaped somewhat like that of a person curled up sleeping on their side. She watched closely for a few seconds, but couldn't see the minute movement one might expect from the expansion and compression of human breathing. There were no sounds. What she was looking at could be a pile of coal or any other of a hundred different inanimate things.

She moved quietly, searching for a weapon. A brick caught her eye. It wasn't the best object to use to defend herself, but it was better than nothing.

Holding the brick in her right hand, she grabbed whatever it was that covered the human-looking bulge. She pulled the cover toward her as she backed away.

She'd moved the cover a few inches when a young

woman with blonde hair sat up, moonlight reflecting off the whites of her eyes. Her face registered fear, but only for a fraction of a second before she relaxed.

"Are you okay?" Angela whispered.

The blonde woman stood and surveyed the room. "Are they here?"

"Who are *they*?"

"I don't know. Not nice people."

"How long have you been here?"

"I'm not sure. I was unconscious when I got here. I've tried to count days, but I can't be positive. Maybe five."

Angela looked around the room. "Did you see them bring me in?"

"No."

"I was unconscious, too. Probably drugged. I don't know how long I've been out."

"I didn't see or hear them bring you in, but they may have taken you somewhere else first."

"You're American, right? What's your name?"

"Emma McCleary."

"I'm Charlene Frank. I was kidnapped in Berlin. Is that where we are now?" Angela used her cover name. She didn't trust anyone.

"I guess we're still in Berlin. That's where I was when they kidnapped me."

"Were you there on holiday?"

"I'm an opera singer. I live in Lűbeck and perform there, but I also travel around the world singing with other opera companies."

Angela wondered if Emma might be older than

she looked. She seemed young to be a professional opera singer. "Where's Lűbeck?"

"It's in Germany. About three hours northwest of Berlin."

"What were you doing in Berlin when you got kidnapped?"

"I'd gone to the refugee camp on the east side of Berlin with a group of singers from Lűbeck. We thought it would be the right thing to do. We wanted to help." Emma's voice caught. "I don't know why they forced me to come here. Maybe because I'm American."

Angela wouldn't share the real reason why she was in Berlin, but Emma seemed so frightened, Angela hugged her. "Maybe together we can find a way to escape."

Emma's body quivered in Angela's grasp. "All we wanted to do was help the refugees."

"What about your friends? Did they get away?"

"I think so. I haven't seen anyone else here until you woke me."

"Did your friends see what happened to you?"

"Yes. When the kidnappers grabbed me, I saw my friends run in all directions to get away. There wasn't much they could have done to help me. I'm sure they went to the police. Maybe the US Embassy, too."

"Are they American also?"

"No. Mostly German. One Italian."

Angela held her close.

Emma sniffed and pulled away. "I'm sorry. I haven't asked about you. Are you okay? I know you're probably scared to death. So far they haven't hurt me.

One of the guards tried to grope me a couple of times, but I've managed to stay away from him. I don't know what will happen if they ask my parents for money. They're poor and my income is very little since I'm just starting my career. You're not American, are you?"

"British. But I'm married to an American." Angela wasn't sure why she added that.

"How did they get you?"

"Same as you, it sounds like. I was trying to help the refugees. I'm a job counselor in Berlin and I was working with companies there to find jobs for refugees. My plan was to help them find work that would allow them to take care of their families and become responsible citizens. On my way to meet with some refugees, a couple of men grabbed me and threw me in a van. I don't know what happened next, but when I woke up here I had the feeling I'd been drugged."

Angela's cover story could be checked out. It'd been set up long before she arrived in Germany three weeks ago. Her assignment was to find the infamous ISIS recruiter Reyaad Amin. Had he found her instead? If so, did he know she had been searching for him?

Angela looked at her wrist and noticed her watch was missing. She'd learned in training to make an inventory of her possessions first chance she got. If she hadn't had to fight the drug fogging her brain she would have thought to do so when she first awoke.

Emma whimpered. "Oh, no."

Angela held her closer "What is it?"

"I was supposed to be in a performance of *Tosca* this weekend. Or . . . was it last weekend?" She cried louder. "My part wasn't big enough for them to have an understudy, but it's too difficult for someone to learn quickly. What will happen now?"

Angela patted her on the back. She wanted to ask Emma more. Like what had happened to her since she got here? What did she eat? Where was the toilet?

The questions would have to wait. Someone had entered the room and was walking rapidly toward them.

***

Liz shouldn't have worried about Samuel. When she told him what Chris had said about needing him to stay at the Hemington house, he didn't ask why. "Yes. I can do that."

"Good. I didn't want to commit until I talked to you. I'm never sure what needs to be done this time of year for the farm."

"Not much. Early February would be the time to shut down everything back home, but here in Georgetown, Texas, we may have had our last freeze. There's still lots to do, but nothing urgent. Michael can take care of it."

Samuel cleared the table while Liz rinsed the dishes.

"I wish I knew more about what to expect," Liz said. "Chris didn't tell me much. Just that he needs our help."

Samuel cleaned the bowl of his pipe with a narrow knife he kept for that purpose. "It's got to be about me niece, Angela, then. Since Chris is being so secretive, I think it best I don't call me brother Harold and ask him what's going on.

"Knowing the nature of Angela's work, I bet no one's told her parents she's MIA, assuming that's what's happened. She didn't tell them she worked for the Secret Intelligence Service until two years ago. And that was because of Chris's prodding."

"Missing in action? Oh, dear. I bet you're right. Chris may have already talked to them. If not, you may want to give Harold and Gina a call while you're there. Still, I agree, it would be best not to alarm them about Angela, certainly not without knowing any details."

He lit his pipe and settled into his easy chair. "Chris is probably protecting them. I'll talk to me brother and let him decide how much to tell his wife."

Michael walked in. "Anything to eat?"

Liz gave him a hug. "Help yourself. It's still on the table. Where've you been?"

Michael loaded his plate the way young people do when eating their grandmother's cooking. "Visiting friends from Austin. A bunch of people I know came to Georgetown for dinner at El Monumento."

Samuel raised his eyes. "And you're still hungry?"

Michael laughed. "I didn't eat much. I had a cola and a small, very tiny, *flauta* appetizer. I knew GiGi would have dinner ready and I didn't want to disappoint her."

Samuel smiled. "Well, sit down, son. I understand. I enjoy her cooking, too."

Liz smiled and hugged Michael again then hugged

Samuel, too. "Michael, we talked it over and we're going to England."

"I knew you would. Can I go? I can help with the computer work, and . . . ."

"You're just beginning your first real job since you graduated from college. I don't want you to do anything to jeopardize it. Besides, Chris said you could work from here to help with the computer stuff."

Michael looked down. "I know. I'd still like to go with you. I've never been anywhere like that."

Samuel held his pipe like a college professor would hold a pointer. "And, we need you to take care of the house and farm while we're gone. Someone's got to feed the animals. Princess will need to be held every night."

Princess' ears twisted as the white poodle jumped into Samuel's lap.

"Yeah, you know we're talking about you, sweetie. She'll need someone to sleep with, too." He turned to Michael. "But your time will come. Do good in your job and save your money. Then you can go anywhere you want."

Liz loved it when Samuel treated Michael like his own son. "You don't have a passport, do you?"

"No. I haven't needed one."

"Get one, son. You never know when you might."

"Okay." Michael pushed a fork packed high with mashed potatoes into his mouth. "I'll take care of things around here, and all. I guess I'll buy some TV dinners."

"You'll have frozen dinners, dear. But not the store-bought kind. Oh, no," Liz said. "I'll cook your favorites before we leave. Good thing we have a large freezer. No telling how long we'll be gone."

After Michael had gone to bed, Liz told Samuel her fears about going to help Chris.

"I met Chris soon after his fiancé had been killed during a robbery. He was one of Percy's college professors and Percy was determined to help him get revenge. I worked with them, doing research and calling on help from friends, but mainly to see that they understood revenge wasn't the answer.

"Turned out we all did some good for the country and Chris worked through his loss in a healthy way. I enjoyed the adventure in England even more." She looked into Samuel's eyes. "But, now, I feel I'm too old for more adventures such as this. Whatever it is."

"Old? You're not old."

"Yes I am. I'm seventy."

"That's merely a number. How do you feel inside?"

"Inside?"

"Yes. How do you see yourself?"

"I don't know. Younger, I guess. Inside, I sometimes think I'm much younger. Forties, fifties, seems like."

"That's what I'm talking about. You're only as old as you feel. I'm older than you if you go by the numbers, but I still work the farm the same as I did when I was twenty."

"You're only seventy-two. That's not much older, number or not. And you have muscles and strength from working the farm."

He smiled. "And you, my dear, are in excellent

shape yourself." He hugged her. "Very good shape."

"Aw, you. I'm overweight and wear baggy clothes, but for some reason you still love me."

He planted a kiss on her lips as if to prove it.

She pushed him away. "But, I'm worried that I may not be strong enough to keep up this time. I don't want to cause something bad to happen to the boys because of my weakness."

"You'll be okay. Chris wouldn't have called for you if he was concerned."

"I guess you're right. But, this will probably be my last time to run off to another country playing detective. I'm content working in my own bookmobile and having you to come home to."

***

"You come."

The man's voice was a growl, but it sounded to Angela to be more bluster than deep feeling. She'd heard the type before. She could overpower him. But if she did, what would happen to Emma? How many cohorts were nearby? She needed more information.

She'd trained for such an event, but real events were never the same as the ones anticipated in class. Angela was groggy from being drugged and she couldn't see because of the dark room. If that wasn't enough, there was a hostage to protect. She had to wait. Study. Then act.

MI6 would be searching for her. Chris, too, she suspected. She'd made him promise not to come for her if she didn't check in with him from time to time. Not because he was a civilian. He'd proven he was a capable investigator. It was for his safety. And she didn't want him to worry unnecessarily.

There were many good reasons why she might be unable to call home periodically and if he had an emergency, her partners would find her. Still, she hoped Chris *would* come get her. That was a new feeling for her. She'd never depended on anyone in her life.

The man pointed his flashlight at Angela. "You. Come now."

CHAPTER THREE

"What?" It took Chris a moment to get back to the here and now. Liz had said something, but he missed it. He'd been a terrible host. Ever since Tex, Liz and Samuel arrived, he hadn't said much. He was too busy thinking about Angela and what he could do to rescue her.

"I said I like your beard. It's filled in nicely."

"Thank you." Chris remembered Liz's good natured jokes about his beard when he first started growing it, back in Austin, before he'd met Angela.

"Do you want me to check the grill?" Liz asked.

"Oh, no . . . I'll do it."

"The rice and salad are ready," she said.

"Good. The lamb shank is cooked. I set it aside away from the charcoal to stay warm. I'll go get it."

From the grill he could see the rock wall separating the garden from the farm land. The last place he'd seen Angela was beyond the rock wall. When the helicopter landed to take her to London for what he'd thought was a routine assignment.

Had he kissed her goodbye? He couldn't remember. Most likely he had. He usually did, but life had become predictable lately. He hoped he'd told her he loved her.

The table was set and everyone took a seat. He straightened his silverware the way he always did. Parallel was his goal. He didn't know why. He looked at Tex to see if his friend had noticed. Evidently. But this time Tex didn't joke about it. Instead, he looked away.

Chris studied the others. Stern. Unsmiling, but loving at the same time. They'd all made sacrifices to be here. They were all waiting for him to bless the food or tell them to eat. But mainly they were probably waiting for him to tell them why he'd called them to help.

"Before I pray, I must tell you why I've asked you here." He paused, gauging his guests' reactions. "Angela is missing and MI6 hasn't told me what's going on." He looked around the table. They waited for more. "I haven't heard from her for thirty-two days."

"Is that unusual, considering she works undercover?" Tex asked.

"Not in itself," Chris said. "There were times when she didn't call home for longer periods."

"So what's different this time?"

"Let me bless this food and I'll tell you all I know while we eat."

They bowed their heads.

Chris paused, took a deep breath and prayed. "Dear Lord, bless these special friends. Watch over Angela. We don't know where she is, but you know her circumstances and you know what we should do. We pray that your plan is for us to find her and bring her home quickly. Lord, we also pray for our safety and strength during our search. And, bless this food. Amen."

He nodded, making eye contact with each person. "Please eat while I tell you what I know. The reason I'm worried this time is because I've picked up chatter from other agencies about an English angel missing in Germany."

Liz drew a deep breath. "Oh, dear God."

Samuel had tears in his eyes. "Me little Angela? Missing? I was afraid of that."

"Is that all you know?" Tex asked.

Chris looked at Tex. "Yes. That's really all I know. That, and the fact Angela's boss is not returning my calls."

Liz held up her fork with a chunk of lamb pointed toward her mouth. "Do you know why she was in Germany?"

"No. I did run across some information indicating the FBI is sending a group of agents to Berlin. It's their IRT, International Response Team, but I don't know if they are going to Berlin because Angela is missing or for some other reason."

Samuel set his fork on the edge of his plate. "Chris, me boy, I know this must be devastating for you. But, I'd be interested to know if you've talked to Harold or Gina lately."

"Angela's mother calls me every week. The last time we talked, she sounded frightened. She didn't talk about it, but I got the feeling she hadn't heard from her daughter in so long she was beginning to guess something might be wrong. I told her it was too early to worry, but I don't think that helped." Chris shook his head. "Sometimes I wish I hadn't urged Angela to tell her parents she worked for MI6. They were happier not knowing, believing she worked for the government tourist office."

"What do you want me to tell them?" Samuel asked. "Or, do you prefer I don't communicate with them at all? We usually talk weekly. They'd get suspicious knowing I was here and didn't at least talk to them."

Chris looked away, scratched his cheek, and looked back at Samuel. "Call them. Harold is your brother and I want you to feel free to tell them what we know. Since that isn't much, there's not a lot to say. Hopefully that will change."

Liz set her water glass on the table. "Let's tell them the truth then. Tell them Angela hasn't checked in lately and we *think* MI6 is worried about her. And, since MI6 won't talk to us, we're going out on our own to find her." She turned to Chris. "That *is* what we're going to do, right?"

Tex and Chris nodded simultaneously. Tex spoke

first. "Yeah. Tell them that. We're *going to* find her."

***

After dinner, they cleaned the kitchen and moved into the family room for coffee and a berry pie Chris's neighbor had baked. Chris added a hearty serving of clotted cream to each slice of pie the way Angela always did.

Chris set up the large white board he'd purchased to make notes for his white-hat hacking jobs. He turned the board where everyone could see it and erased the computer notes. "Let's use this to list ways to find Angela. Call out any ideas that come to mind."

"Brainstorming, right?" Tex said.

Chris picked up a grease pen. "Yes. And, that means there's no such thing as a bad suggestion. Only after we list all ideas will we begin to whittle them down."

"Before we look for solutions," Liz said, "we need to learn everything you know about Angela's disappearance."

"Right," Samuel said. "Tell us what you've found out so far."

"There's not much more than what I've already said. And what I know was obtained illegally, so I can't use it to talk to anyone in the government."

"Illegally?" Liz raised her brows. "Michael said you designed the software on the US Defense Department's computers to keep hackers out."

"I did. I do a lot of work for them, but lately I've

been looking into places not covered by my contract to try to learn what happened to Angela. I've also hacked into the computers at MI6 and the FBI without permission."

"So," Samuel said, "we could all be arrested for . . . for what?"

"Espionage?" Tex asked.

Chris cleared his throat and everyone turned to him. "Listen. No matter what you call it, it's illegal. Still, I'm willing to take a chance to find Angela. If you feel uncomfortable with this, I'll understand. What I learn from hacking into government computers will not be misused. And, so far, I'm the only one they could blame."

Liz got up and looked at the white board. "I say we do it."

Tex turned toward Chris. "I'm in. Whatever it takes."

"I'll probably lose my green card and have to stay in England permanently," Samuel said, "but count me in, too."

Liz's eyebrows raised as she smiled. "Don't worry, dear. If you stay, I'm staying with you."

Chris looked at each person. "Okay. Thank you all for sticking with me. Now, here's what I learned poking around. Angela was abducted in Berlin near a refugee camp. Her partner saw her being forced into a van. He followed, but soon lost them. There was no license plate on the vehicle."

Chris made notes about Berlin and the refugee center on the white board.

"You were going to tell us why she was in Berlin," Tex said.

"From what I could glean from partially-encrypted messages between the Americans and the British, she was supposed to be observing Syrian refugees at the camp there. She had a cover story about being sent there by some international company headquartered in London to help refugees find jobs."

Chris added notes on the board about Angela's cover story.

"Hmm," Liz said. "Can we learn the exact spot where she was abducted? If so, I suggest we go there and trace her steps back from that point. She must have alerted someone, made somebody suspicious."

"We know where she was grabbed," Chris said.

Liz continued. "What time? Do we know where she stayed the night before she was kidnapped . . . does she speak Syrian . . . what is the language of Syria?" She returned to the spot on the sofa she'd claimed earlier.

Chris made notes as Liz talked. "Arabic is the primary language."

"Does Angela speak Arabic?" Samuel asked.

"I don't know," Chris said. "I have heard her speaking in other languages on the phone, but I wouldn't know Arabic if she spoke it."

"What about Liz's other questions?" Samuel asked.

Chris looked up. He reviewed Liz's input, *what time was she kidnapped, where did she stay the night before she was taken.* "As I mentioned, her partner was an eyewitness to her kidnapping. I've got an address, date and time, and comments about the kidnapper's vehicle. I haven't heard where Angela stayed the night before she was abducted, but her partner would know that, too. He probably won't talk to me. Not because he doesn't want to, but because the agency won't let him. I'll dig around the MI6 computer files to find what we need."

Liz shook her head. "Dear Chris. I'm so sorry. It's a good thing you know how to get into that computer. Back home, in a situation like this, I would call my friends in the police department to get answers. That's not going to work in Germany."

Chris nodded. "I know. It won't matter much. I doubt if the police know anything. If MI6 coordinated with the German government, it'd be to ask them to stay out of the way. You bring up a good point though. It might not be feasible this time, but in the past you were our government contact, the one who knew police chiefs in several cities and a couple of countries. You were also good at getting equipment and supplies."

"And money," Tex added.

"Yes," Chris said. "Let's make a list of each of our special talents." He took a blue pen and wrote everyone's first name at the top of a column. Under Liz's name he wrote "Resource coordinator, government contact." Under Tex's name he jotted, "Disguises, conman, computer skills, wheelchair."

Tex rolled up to the white board and jabbed a finger at his column. "Wheelchair? What's that mean? That's not a specialty. It's a necessity."

Chris grinned. "For our job, it's a specialty. It makes you look less threatening. And gets you into places the rest of us can't go. Remember that time in Albuquerque?"

Tex smiled. "Oh, yeah. That's true. The wheelchair came in handy in El Paso, too."

Under his own name, Chris wrote, "Computer skills."

"Don't forget your photographic memory," Tex said.

Chris added "eidetic memory" to his list, but to him it didn't mean much. Growing up, he thought his so-called photographic memory was normal. It was a surprise to learn that most people couldn't recall everything they'd read.

"Oh, yeah, I forgot you call it *eidetic*," said Tex.

"What about me?" Samuel asked. "What can I do to help?"

"I'd like you to man the base camp," Chris said. "If Angela somehow makes her way home, or sends a message, someone needs to be here. Will you do that?"

"Of course," Samuel said. "Whatever you want."

Chris added Samuel's name to the board with Hemington contact under it. When Chris turned around, Liz mouthed "thank you" where only he could see it. He tried not to smile. He hadn't assigned Samuel to a safer job for Liz. It was a necessary job and her husband was the best choice.

Liz walked to the white board. "If I'm gonna be the resource coordinator, let's talk about transportation. We're going to need a van or something to get around."

She looked toward Chris. "I assume you think we should go where Angela was last seen, right? We need a vehicle large enough for all of us while allowing us to move about without attracting attention."

"Right," Tex said. "Something with a wheelchair lift would be nice."

Liz nodded. "That's what I meant by saying we need a vehicle that's big enough for all of us."

Chris made a note on the board about an inconspicuous vehicle with a wheelchair lift.

Samuel cleared his voice. "I don't know a lot about any of this, but it doesn't seem plausible for there to be a vehicle like that that's inconspicuous, especially in an EU country like Germany."

"If we had the money . . . " Chris wasn't sure whether he should bring it up or not. The cost would be prohibitive. "We could get a van loaded with electronic equipment to help in our search. Computers, Wi-Fi routers, surveillance gear." He paused. "If we could afford it." He added the equipment to the board.

"Hmm," Liz said. "I can call Brian. After that last adventure, he promised to provide whatever we needed whenever we wanted it."

"Is that the millionaire friend I've heard you talking about?" Samuel asked Liz.

"*Multi*-millionaire," Tex said.

Liz smiled. "Karen and Brian Donelson live in California now. He's helped us financially in many ways. He loves to set things right by rewarding good and catching bad guys. I'll call him and see what he can do about a vehicle for us. I'll tell him about all that other technical stuff you mentioned, but if we can get a basic van, I'll be happy. We could add the other. Also, Chris, you may have to tell him about the computer equipment you want. You know how I am about that techy junk."

"Thanks, Liz," Chris said. "Anything you can do will be appreciated. I think we need to head to Germany tomorrow, so tell Brian we'll call him back as soon as we have an address there."

"Will do," Liz said. She looked around the room. "Before I call him, are there any more resources we need?"

"Does anyone here speak German?" Samuel asked.

No one said a word.

Samuel continued. "If it was me heading out on such a serious journey as I'm hearing this is, I'd want to have someone with me who is fluent in the language. Sure, most Germans speak English, unless they grew up in East Germany. The ones there speak Russian. Still, it'd be nice to be able to read the signs, understand TV and radio, and talk to people in their own language."

Chris nodded toward Samuel and added the idea to the white board. "Good points. I know many German words, but I don't know enough to put together a coherent sentence to communicate with a German-speaking person. We probably should hire a guide. It'll be costly and we'll have to find someone we can trust."

"I guess we could all kick in to help with the expenses." Tex paused. "I'll have to check with Jane."

Chris shook his head. "Oh, no. This is my problem. I don't expect you to pay for anything. Angela and I have some savings . . . we've been talking about having a child . . . so, we've put some aside for when she has to take off work."

"Oh, no you don't," Liz said. "I'm the resource coordinator. I'll take care of it."

Samuel turned his head toward Liz and took in a deep breath followed by a noticeable gulp. "Are you sure?"

"No," Liz said. "Not us. I mean I'll ask Brian about it. If we need more financial backing than he's comfortable giving, he has friends who also love to finance missions such as this. Don't worry. They'll be glad to kick in whatever we need."

"Thank you, Liz. Good idea, Samuel," Chris said.

Liz turned to go back to her seat, then stopped. "Is it okay to tell Brian what's going on? That Angela is missing?"

Chris took several more seconds than usual to answer. "Yes. He needs to know."

Liz turned her gaze to Chris. "Good. Is there anything else I should ask for?"

"That's all I can think of now. Anyone else?" He looked around the room. "Okay. I'll make train reservations. We'll head for Berlin tomorrow."

Liz pulled out her phone. "Okay. While you do that, I'll call Brian. Anyone know what time it is in California?"

CHAPTER FOUR

Angela's body stiffened as the man pushed her across the room. She looked back to see if Emma was okay, but all she saw was the young woman's shadow. Angela was trained to handle abductions, and she'd used the techniques successfully more than once.

This situation was different. She was weak from whatever they'd used to dope her. She didn't know where she was or how long she'd been there. And, a supposed civilian hostage was involved. Angela couldn't jeopardize Emma's safety in case the woman was really who she said.

"Go that way." The man shoved her toward a door that gave way to her body as she bumped into it.

Angela scanned the room as her eyes adjusted to more light. They were in a bar. Not an active one. It probably hadn't been open for business for months, maybe years.

The Germans would call it a Rathskeller, like an English pub. Except a Rathskeller was usually in a cellar. There was a huge wooden bar, now cluttered with empty bottles and food-serving pans. Tables and chairs, some strewn about the room. Empty bottles, plates, saucers, broken glasses and a variety of forks, spoons, and knives littered the floor.

She looked around. The front windows were boarded over with plywood sheets, making it impossible to see what was outside. A sturdy chain connected by a steel lock held double doors in place.

She walked slowly, determined to take it all in and memorize her surroundings. Everything she learned might be used for her escape. There wasn't time for human fears about what might happen next.

Her thoughts turned to why had she been kidnapped and if they'd figured out who she was. She hadn't carried ID, but she had . . . she'd forgotten to check the bug. Was it still there? Was it working? She smiled. Surely, her friends knew where she was.

*****

"We're eight hours ahead of California." Chris looked at his phone. "It's 6:30 PM here, so it's 10:30 in the morning there."

"Good time to call Brian." Liz started to walk away, but stopped and looked at the notes Chris had made on the white board. "What if I need you to explain that special equipment you'd like?"

Chris smiled. "Just let me know. I'm doing the train reservations online, and I can pause anytime."

Liz went to one corner of the room to make her call. Chris opened his laptop and started punching keys.

Tex rolled up to Chris. "How far is it from here to Berlin by train?"

"Twelve and half hours."

"Wouldn't it be better to fly?"

Chris continued to type. "Not really. The train takes longer than the flight itself, but there's much less hassle taking the train. The time it takes to get to the airport and go through security adds up. Besides, going on the train will give us more time to talk and plan."

"Chris," Liz called from across the room. "Come talk to Brian."

He took the phone from Liz. She walked back to talk to the others.

"Hello," Chris said.

"Hi, Chris. I'm sorry to hear Angela is missing. Karen and I will pray for you and the team to find her and bring her home safely."

"Thank you. I appreciate the prayers . . . and your help."

"Liz told me about the vehicle and the German guide you need. She said you also have a need for some special gear. Fill me in on what you're talking about."

"Sure. First, it would be nice to have Wi-Fi in the

van if possible. I can bring my laptop, but it'd be faster if we didn't have to go through the phone company."

"Wi-Fi." From the way he said it, Brian was probably making notes. "That won't be a problem. What else?"

"There's one thing I haven't told the rest. Angela has an RFID chip embedded in her bra strap. I don't have a method to read the chips, but there must be some technique we can use to locate her by finding the chip. I suspect I can learn her frequency number by hacking into the agency's files. Given enough time, I could probably build an RFID reader. Right now, though, my goal is to learn enough about RFID technology to tell you exactly what we need."

"No need. my friends will know what will work. Whatever an RFID reader is, I'll have it in the van by the time you get to Germany. Anything else?"

Chris thanked God for Brian. "Thank you. I know this is adding up quickly, so stop me if we ask for too much."

"Go ahead. I'm listening."

"We need some special communication devices that will fit in our ears so we can talk to each other when we are separated. It's expensive, but the best I've seen is a wireless IFB Inductive Earpiece along with the accessories. It's the type used by news anchors and stage actors."

"I can see how that could be handy to have. I'll see what I can do."

"It wasn't on the list, but I'd love to have a small drone with a webcam so we can look around without putting anyone in harm's way."

"Drone with camera. Anything else?"

"Uh, I don't know if this is possible, but it'd be nice to have two pistols."

"I'll see what my friends say. If I can manage it, do you have a preferred type?"

"Glock 19 for me and a Colt Model 191 semi-automatic for Tex."

"That it?"

"Yes."

"Okay. Liz told me you're leaving by train tomorrow, so I should have everything ready when you get there. Text me your hotel info. If my Belgian contacts have questions, they can talk to you on the train. Tell Liz goodbye for me. I want to get started on this right away."

"Will do. And . . . thanks. This means a lot to me. To all of us."

"It's important to me, too. There are many people around the globe who are interested in doing the right thing. People who will help in the field and others who will finance what is being done. Be safe."

After disconnecting, Chris called Michael in Georgetown. "I've got a job for you."

"What's up?"

"Angela is wearing an RFID chip and I don't know anything about the technology. Brian's getting us a reading device, but I need you to do some research and see how we can use it to find Angela."

"On it."

***

Every so often, the man behind Angela pushed her in the middle of the back, urging her on, forcing her to go forward. He was either stupid or wasn't concerned about her because she was a petite woman. Otherwise, he wouldn't have signaled his position to her by making contact with her back.

She deliberately stopped at times to see if he would prod her again. There were many ways to take him down, and she had used most of them in real situations. The one she favored was to render him unconscious with a choke hold. She could do it quickly, before he had time to use the weapon on her.

Problem was, she didn't know who was nearby, who might run to his aid. She also didn't know what would happen to Emma as a result.

"Stop," he said, one hand on her shoulder.

She froze in place.

"Turn around and take this."

She faced him. The gun in his right hand drooped and pointed toward the floor instead of her. He'd be easy to overpower. In his other hand was what looked like a scarf.

She understood what he wanted, but she didn't move. This gave her time to look him over, judge his strength, his attention, determine how best to protect herself and get away. A difficult goal because of the way she felt. She was still unsteady and nauseous. Not the best time to take out an armed enemy with only her hands. What if they kept drugging her so she couldn't fight back?

He pushed the scarf toward her and pointed his gun at her. "Take!"

Angela refused.

He glared. His eyes grew so large they seemed to fill the top part of his face. Angela could see the veins in his head pulsing. He was furious. She wanted to laugh, but there was no reason to make him madder.

"Liliane!"

From the sound of his voice, he wasn't concerned about anyone outside hearing. Where were they that no one would be alarmed by such an outburst? This was once a place to drink and eat. There would be people walking by or in the neighborhood. Or, maybe not. Maybe the place closed because there were no customers. That reminded her of the airport refugee camp. Could it be possible she was still in the same area where she was kidnapped?

An older woman in a long lavender dress and white hijab entered the room. She spoke in Arabic and the man with the gun responded in Arabic. Angela thanked God she was fluent in the language. A few years ago, MI6 had offered incentives to agents who learned Arabic. She was glad she'd taken the class.

She learned the man's name was Sayid. He wanted Liliane to force the infidel to cover her head with the hijab he offered. They argued briefly before Liliane took the hijab from him and walked toward Angela.

Angela guarded her reactions, not wanting them to know she understood what had been said. Why did they want her to put on the hijab? Was it to make Sayid more comfortable, or were they planning to move her somewhere and didn't want to draw attention from anyone on the street.

Still woozy from the drug they'd given her, Angela decided she wouldn't wear the head covering. Not to be stubborn, but because she wanted to stay close to Emma. They would have a better chance of escaping if they worked together. If she put on the hijab, she might be taken away.

Liliane walked toward Angela with no emotion showing. When she reached Angela, she managed a slight smile as she touched Angela's dark brown hair.

"So . . . so lovely." Liliane used her fingers to comb through Angela's hair.

Angela ignored Liliane and fixed her gaze on Sayid who remained nearby, watching.

Liliane held the hijab open and moved forward. Angela grabbed the head cover and threw it to the floor. It landed on top of a pile of empty bottles and refuse.

Liliane's eyes widened, but she turned from Angela and looked instead at Sayid as if fearing his reaction. Angela was right. He walked up to Liliane and slapped her in the face. The impact of his open hand against her cheek was enough to knock her to the floor.

Angela didn't move, but wondered what she would do if he tried to smack her next. Was he hitting Liliane because she failed to get Angela to wear the hijab or was it to force Angela to either wear it or watch Liliane get punished more?

As Sayid walked toward her with the gun still in his hand, Angela decided she had to protect herself without giving away the fact she was trained in hand-to-hand combat. If she used her agent skills, and lost this battle, they'd know she was not a job counselor from England. He picked up the hijab, rubbed it against his dirty jeans, and extended to her.

She stood frozen in place with her eyes locked on him measuring his body reactions for any indication of what might come next.

"Nizar!"

A man wearing a gun belt came running into the room with a pistol in his hand.

Angela again considered various responses she could make, but before she needed them, she heard Sayid tell Nizar to return the infidel to the locked room.

She'd won this time without giving away information about who she was. Now if only she could learn why she had been kidnapped.

CHAPTER FIVE

Liz and Tex slept most of the time as the train traveled from Bath to Berlin. Chris couldn't have slept if he'd wanted to. Not with the thoughts that continuously moved through his mind. Where was his wife? Was she in pain? What would life be like without her? He deleted that last thought. Instead, he obsessed on how remarkable it was he'd found her and married her in the first place.

Brian called about the time they entered Hanover. "I think you'll be pleasantly surprised," Brian said. "My Belgian friends are heading for Berlin as we speak. They've obtained a fully-loaded minibus and it should be at the hotel when you get there."

"That's wonderful." Chris knew the effort that must have gone into securing the vehicle and electronic equipment so quickly. It wouldn't have been possible without Brian's help. "Did they know anything about RFID readers?" He hoped he wasn't asking too much.

"Yes." Brian's voice didn't sound as if he was put off by the question. If anything, he seemed happy, maybe pleased he could help.

"Thank God," Chris said.

"You'll find a variety of RFID readers, enough to match whatever Angela might be wearing."

"That's perfect. Anything else I should know?"

"I think you'll be able to figure out how everything works, but they said they'd leave operating manuals in the minibus. Call me if you have questions and I'll put you in touch with my Belgian friends. They also recommended a guide. One they have used for business purposes before. He speaks English and German and he knows the city and how to protect you and your information."

"What's his name?"

"Hmm, he didn't say. They said he'd look for you at the hotel. His services are paid for two weeks. If you need him longer, let me know."

"Okay. I hope it doesn't take that long." Chris couldn't bear another day without Angela, much less two weeks. To be honest, it wasn't being separated that bothered him. They'd learned to cope with being apart because of her job. It was not knowing where she was . . . or if she was okay . . . or alive. He aborted those thoughts quickly, wanting to think only about finding her alive and well.

Brian's voice brought him back to the present. "I

don't think it'll take that long either, but thought it best to have the guide for the two weeks just in case."

"Thanks, Brian. Liz and Tex are napping and I'd rather not wake them until we get into Berlin. They're still a little jet-lagged. I'll tell them what all you've done and I'm sure they'll be as appreciative as I am. There aren't enough words to tell you how much your help means to me, to all of us."

"I understand. I hope taking care of the logistics will free your mind to find Angela. I've kept up with you over the years and I'm proud of what you've accomplished. All of you."

"Thanks." Brian's comments made Chris think of his parents and how he hadn't yet told them about Angela's disappearance. "Could I ask you for one more favor?"

"Certainly. Just name it." Brian sounded as if he meant it.

"Would you mind getting hold of my parents in Long Beach and letting them know what's going on? I want them to know, but I don't want to talk to them now. Especially, my mother. She gets so upset, I'll feel guilty when I should be concentrating on finding Angela. Do you mind?"

"Of course not. I understand. Text me the contact info and I'll take care of it. But, you're going to need to talk to them soon."

"I will. I want to give them time to absorb what's going on before I call them."

"Don't worry. I'll take care of it."

Chris said goodbye as the train slowed for the

Berlin station.

***

When Angela got back to what Sayid called "the lockable room," Emma wasn't there. Since there was little chance the young opera singer had escaped, Angela concluded that one or more terrorists had taken Emma away for some reason.

The significance of that conclusion was an increase in the number of known enemies. Angela had met Sayid, Liliane, and Nizar, and all three were with her when Emma disappeared. How many more were there? She'd have to ask Emma if she knew. If Emma returned.

While searching the room, Angela found bottled water and sandwiches. The sandwiches were sealed in cellophane paper and the water bottle appeared to have the original seal in place. Still, she knew there were ways to put drops into what appeared to be unopened containers.

The captors would want them healthy for whatever they intended to do with them, so she wasn't concerned that the water and food contained poison. But she couldn't rule out the use of drugs to keep them in a weakened condition.

What did the kidnappers have in mind for them? Emma thought she might be offered up for ransom, but did she really know? Kidnapping young women wasn't usually for ransom. Instead, it helped fuel a multi-million-dollar global sex-slave industry. Some ended up as suicide bombers, but that took a larger amount of brainwashing.

Angela thought of the talk she'd had with Chris before they were married. One of many long talks that led to their marriage. They'd spoken of children, of being parents someday. She hadn't wanted to give up her work.

He said he'd be mother and father. Her response was crystal clear. "A child needs a mother *and* a father." He persisted and said she could be a mother much of the time. "I know you need to be able to leave in a hurry for unknown lengths of time. When that happens, I'll be mother and father."

She finally had to be honest and tell him her fear. "I'm not sure it would be good for the child for me to leave it alone so much."

That's when he asked the question that haunted her now in a locked room in a Berlin pub. "Are you afraid becoming a mother would soften you and make you more vulnerable during a time when you need to be tough?"

Angela knew now she hadn't understood the impact of being a mother. A mother would do anything to protect her child. She felt her abdomen for the hundredth time since her captivity. She had to survive and get back to Chris. To do so meant varying her usual way of reacting in dangerous situations. If that was possible.

***

The hotel Chris had booked for the team was a few blocks from Angela's last known location, the spot where she'd been kidnapped, according to MI6. Had she stayed in the same hotel? He didn't know, but he wanted to find out.

The front of the building was obscured by construction barriers, like so many structures they'd seen along their walk from the train station. Chris hesitated to go into what looked like a hard-hat area, so he pulled out the hotel confirmation to double check the address. Before he had a chance to study the information, a bellhop ran out and pointed the way through the maze to an elaborate, old-country style lobby.

"*Kommen auf diese Weise bitte.*"

"Come this way, please." He repeated in English.

When Liz got to the bellhop, she gave him her usual hug. He recovered faster than some, grinned, and hugged back.

Chris smiled at Liz and the bellhop as he walked toward the check-in desk. He stopped and looked around, wondering if Angela had been there.

Tex rolled up to where Chris stood. "You okay, Doc? You look like you've seen a ghost."

"I'm all right. Thinking about Angela, wondering if this could be where she stayed before . . . "

"I know it must be difficult, Doc, but we'll get some answers soon. I promise." Tex gave Chris a soft punch on the shoulder.

The desk clerk checked them in and gave Chris a large sealed envelope with Chris's name handwritten on the front. He ripped the envelope open while they were standing in the lobby. Inside he found a typewritten note along with a vehicle key. He scanned the paper and stuffed it in his pocket.

When he looked up, Tex and Liz were staring at him. He raised the envelope. "I've got some information to share with you, but I'd rather not talk in the lobby. How about getting together in my room in ten minutes? Room 303. Is that okay?"

They both nodded and headed toward the elevator. Chris could tell they were lethargic from the long train ride. He hoped he could pep them up. They'd be surprised when they saw the minibus.

***

The remodeling he'd observed at the hotel's entrance hadn't reached his room. It reminded him of the hotel rooms in movies set in the late 1940s and early 1950s, around the time Berlin was being rebuilt after World War II.

It was stark, without color. The furniture consisted of heavy wooden pieces dry and flaking from lack of care. The white concrete walls were adorned simply with framed black and white drawings of trees and mountains. On the bed was a white duvet, untucked, and at a slight angle with the bed frame. He straightened it.

Liz and Tex arrived before Chris unpacked. He moved his suitcase to give Liz a place to sit on the bed. Chris took the one chair in the room. Tex, as usual, brought his own chair.

"Talk to us, Professor," Tex said, with a smile reminding Chris of when Tex was one of his students at Austin Community College.

Chris pulled the page from the envelope and read.

On behalf of Mr Brian Donelson of California, U.S.A., we are pleased to provide the vehicle and equipment described herein to assist in your investigation.

We discussed various types of vans to house the surveillance equipment you requested, with consideration given to not drawing attention to the vehicle itself. We considered utility company trucks, postal vans, and the like. Then I remembered Mr Donelson mentioning how you used mobile libraries for such excursions in the past. You will be happy to learn we found the perfect vehicle. It is larger than we originally planned, but small enough to be maneuverable in most situations.

As you will see, half of the vehicle is a working library and can be used to make your stay at any location easily explainable. The back half of the minibus was once a supply area for the library and now contains the equipment you requested. That portion cannot be seen from the library half when the interior door (which is a shelf of books) is closed. The door can be opened and locked into place when desired.

There is wheelchair access to the back end of the

vehicle for use as needed. If a patron asks to use it, there is a sign in German saying the lift is temporarily out of order. You'll find Germans tend to obey signs and do not get too excited about such inconveniences. We've also included a sign saying the bookmobile is closed for when you don't want patrons entering the front of the vehicle.

The diesel minibus is a Mercedes and has seen better days, but the engine has been replaced and runs like new. The red and cream color of the vehicle identifies it as belonging to the city of Darmstadt.

I'm sure you can come up with an explanation of why the bus has strayed so far from its hometown. I've been told you are all resourceful when it comes to misdirection. For your information, we purchased the vehicle from the city library in Darmstadt, and we have left you copies of the transfer of ownership in case questions are asked by the authorities in Berlin. I don't expect that to happen, however.

Chris paused and looked at Liz. As he expected she had a grin on her face.

Liz jumped up and hugged him. "A bookmobile! Isn't that sweet."

Tex nodded. "Sweet. Now tell us about the computers."

Chris looked down at the print out and resumed reading.

In the back section of the vehicle, which we have been referring to as the Operations Control Center, you will find two state-of-the-art computers fully equipped with software we thought you might find useful. The computers are connected to the outside world through a satellite dish installed on top of the mobile library. A Wi-Fi router provides access for all the devices in the minibus plus any you may have brought with you.

"Now that's what I'm talking about," Tex said, bumping a fist in his hand.

Chris looked up from the message he had been reading. "This next part may not make sense without providing additional information first. I know that Angela wears an RFID chip in her clothing, so I asked Brian for RFID readers." He looked down and continued to read.

You will find two RFID readers as well. One is a passive reader and the other an active reader. None of the personnel here have experience with these devices, but the specialist we talked to said one or the other will meet your needs.

However, he also said you must be no more than thirty feet from where the RFID tag is located. I am sorry I cannot help more with this. However, if you discover a need for more equipment, for whatever purpose, contact me anytime.

I am familiar with the personal communication

devices you requested, having used them on several occasions myself. Again, there is a distance concern. Unlike the usual Bluetooth remotes hanging out of people's ears, these devices are made to look like the inside of ears and are difficult to detect by sight. Not impossible, however. And clearly noticeable up close. You may find the operating manuals useful if this equipment is new to you.

Chris paused again and looked up. "We're going have to learn to use the communications gear, especially since we'll be separated on the minibus, some of us in the bookmobile area and some in the operations area."

Liz made a face as if she'd bitten a piece of lemon. "Yuk. I don't think I'm going to like sticking something in my ear. At my age, it's too much like wearing a hearing aid."

Tex looked at her with raised brows. "What's wrong with hearing aids?"

"Nothing. My doctor has been bugging me to get tested. I'm too young for such things."

Tex looked at Chris and they both smiled.

"I saw that," Liz said.

Chris continued reading.

We have included two large drones and six small ones. All are equipped with cameras and the ability to transmit live to the vehicle's control room. I suggest you save one of the large drones for backup in case something happens to the other. The small ones are made to look like flying beetles. They are battery operated and only run for a short time. However, they transmit live views of what they see and are handy for getting into small openings.

We added several cameras with flexible lenses that let you look under doors and such. I think you'll find them useful.

After lengthy debate, we have included the pistols you requested along with a supply of ammunition for each. We were told by Mr Donelson that you can be trusted to use them carefully, and only for defense.

Chris looked up from the letter and scanned the faces of his friends. "That's it except for the contact information."

Liz crossed her arms in front of her body and made her angry sound. "Harrumph. We shouldn't have a need for guns. In fact, there's never a need for them in my view."

Tex spun his wheelchair around, clearly in preparation to defend his right to carry a weapon. Before he opened his mouth, Chris got his attention and signaled him to not respond. "Don't worry, Liz. The guns are for emergencies only. We won't take them out of the minibus unless we anticipate some defensive need. Most of the time, they'll be stowed somewhere in the vehicle."

Tex's defensiveness abated. "Speaking of the minibus, can we go look at it now?"

"Can we?" asked Liz. She apparently decided to drop the subject of guns.

Chris stood. "Sure, let's go check out our new toys. Then we'll go get something to eat." He didn't like taking time away from the search, but knew he had to keep his body fueled and figure out a plan of action.

CHAPTER SIX

Angela sat on the floor near where she'd first discovered the young opera singer and mentally clicked off the possibilities of where the woman might be. The captors might be interrogating Emma to learn more about Emma's family. Information they could use to get a ransom. They may have moved her to another location. She may have gotten away. Angela decided that wasn't likely. Based on what she'd seen of Emma's physical and mental condition, the odds the woman had escaped were next to nil.

Angela had yet to eat or drink the water she'd found. To get her mind off her hunger, and to help retain her body strength, Angela did pushups until she felt faint. Her hunger pangs increased from the exercise. She was so hungry she wondered if she'd been knocked out longer than she thought. If so, the kidnappers could have moved her away from the area where they grabbed her.

Emma thought they were in Berlin and the closed business and lack of foot traffic nearby indicated they could be near the airport refugee camp. Angela couldn't be sure.

The lost watch was significant. It wasn't merely a time piece. It was a GPS device made to look like a watch. It tracked her location and transmitted the GPS coordinates via satellite. Hopefully some kidnapper was wearing it now and would soon be found. Perhaps he'd lead the agents to where she was being held.

What else was missing?

She checked the pockets of her slacks. Empty. She'd had close to 200 Euros in twenties when she left the hotel. All gone. Her hotel key card was missing, too. She could understand them taking the money, but why the key card? It had the name of the hotel on it, but not the room number. Or, did they simply take everything she had? What else had been in her pockets? A phone.

It wasn't her agency phone. She'd left that, her agency ID, and credit cards in the hotel room safe. The phone she'd had with her was a burner phone, one she could use for any reason without anyone knowing who she worked for. It was gone.

She reached under her blouse and found the RFID chip was in place. Good. They hadn't found that. The chip was an active unit with a long-life battery and made to look like the catch for her bra. She hoped it was working, but it had such a short range it wouldn't do much good if the agency didn't know where to look.

The hunger pains became more severe and she reached for the sandwich. As she started to open the package, Emma sauntered in the door, reminding Angela of an actor walking slowly across the stage while knowing the audience was watching.

***

They found the minibus parked around the corner from the hotel. As described, the bottom was a faded red that reminded Chris of the color of tomato soup. The top half of the vehicle was creamy white. On the front of the vehicle, above the windshield, *Fahrbücherei* was painted in bold black letters. Chris knew *Bücherei* meant library and *Fahren* was the German word for drive or travel. Together, it was a way of saying a library on wheels or mobile library. On the side was *Stadtbücherei Darmstadt*, or Darmstadt City Library.

There were two doors on the passenger's side, one in the front and one in the back. A wheelchair lift covered most of the rear of the minibus.

Chris used the key from the envelope to unlock the front door. He and Liz entered. Clearly, the vehicle had a few miles on it, but it didn't appear unloved. The driver's seat was covered in leather, or some leather lookalike, that appeared to be new. Book shelves packed with German-language books covered three walls.

"Nice," Liz said. "I hope no one expects me to read

any of these books."

"What's in there?" Tex was still on the street. "What'd you find?"

Liz poked her head out. "It's a bookmobile. All the books are in German, though. That's going to make it difficult for me to recommend books to patrons the way I usually do."

Chris slipped by Liz and stepped outside. "Hopefully we won't have any patrons. The books are to give us a reason to be here in such a large vehicle."

Liz leaned out the door and held a book out for all to see. "Look. I found one by my favorite thriller author."

"Who's that?" Chris asked.

"Bonnie Hearn Hill." Liz paused. "The book title is *Ich wünsche dass sie mich vermisst.*" She clobbered the pronunciation.

"Let me see that." Chris's brow furrowed while he looked up the German translation in his memory. He couldn't read or speak German, but he had once read an entire German to English dictionary for fun. He retained much of it because of his special memory. "I . . . wish . . . that . . . you . . . me . . . missed."

Liz nodded. "Yes. That's her latest book. *I Wish You Missed Me.* So, this is one book I can recommend. Maybe that German translator we're getting will help, in case we do have patrons stop by for books."

"Good idea." Chris turned to Tex. "Let's check to see how the wheelchair lift works, Tex."

They walked to the back of the minibus and pulled a lever that lowered a flat metal plate to street level.

"Now you're talking." Tex rolled onto the plate and locked his wheels.

Chris reversed the lever to lift the metal plate up to where it was even with the floor of the bus. After Tex had entered, Chris closed the wheelchair door.

Liz and Chris entered through the rear side door. Chris touched the wall closest to the front of the vehicle.

"Remember," he said, "there's a way we can push this wall aside to allow us to go back and forth between the library section and the control center without exiting the vehicle first. We'll need to put up the closed sign before we move the wall, though. We wouldn't want the patrons, if we get any, to see the control center."

"Excellent." Liz smiled. "That'll be much easier than climbing those steps on both ends of the bus."

"We probably should put up the sign that says the lift is out of order and leave it up," Tex said.

"Hmm," Chris said, "good idea."

In the middle of the operations control center was a large round desk with two computers. Chris sat in front of one of the computers and turned it on. "The computers are both new and top of the line. I don't know if they are tied into the internet yet, but I'm about to find out. Those friends of Brian seem to have thought of everything."

Tex rolled left, then right, looking around the area. "Yeah. Do you see any drones? That's what I'd like to find. A computer is a computer, but I've never seen a beetle-sized drone."

Chris joined the search. "It sounds interesting. I hope we get a chance to use one."

Liz moved to the corner of the minibus, beside the desk. "Here's a bunch of boxes. Maybe the drones are in one of them."

"Let's find out," Tex said, sounding more like a child on Christmas morning than the father of two.

Liz smiled. "Hold your horses."

Sure enough, the first two boxes contained drones that were about a foot long and a foot wide. Liz pulled one out of its box. "Are these the large ones or the small ones? They're smaller than the ones used by the military. They're even smaller than that one you built when we were in England searching for the missing bookmobile fund."

"I think what you have there are considered the large ones," Chris said. "Remember, he said the small ones are the size of a beetle."

"How big is a beetle?" Tex asked.

"The Titan beetle is one of the largest beetles." Chris sounded as if he was reading from an encyclopedia. "It is six and a half inches in length."

Liz opened another box. It held all six of the beetle-like drones. "Ah, here they are. Yukky. They look real, but I can't imagine they can fly very far." She pushed the box toward Tex.

Tex took the box and reached for one of the miniatures.

Chris tightened his grip on the container. "Let's wait until morning. There's a whole stack of operation manuals to read before we play with these toys. Let's

SIDNEY W. FROST

go eat and then get an early start tomorrow."

Tex didn't move toward the lift. "Weren't you gonna check that computer?"

"I did." Chris typed and clicked. "It's connected to the internet. That's enough for now." He positioned the wheelchair lift.

"I need some time to wash up," Liz said. "Okay if we meet in the lobby in about thirty minutes?"

The men nodded as Chris helped Tex with the wheelchair lift.

Chris headed back to the control center. "I forgot to put up the lift out-of-order sign. I'll meet you two in the lobby in thirty minutes."

With Tex and Liz gone, he found the sign and what had been on his mind since they first entered the minibus. The manual for the RFID reader. He scanned the instructions, found the device and turned it on. His heart missed a beat thinking the equipment could locate Angela.

He waited.

Nothing. It was too much to think she was close enough to where the bus was parked to show up on the reader, but he had to try. He wished he could be sure he was using the equipment correctly, and it was working.

He looked around in the box and found a test RFID chip was included to test the equipment. He flipped the switch on. The reader lit up and beeped. That meant the reader was working. He turned off the test chip and the beeping stopped. That meant Angela wasn't close by.

The minibus back door opened. "Chris? You still there?" It was Tex. "Didn't you say thirty minutes?"

"Is it time already? I was reading the users' manual for some of the equipment."

"Liz is ready to eat. So am I."

"Okay." He wanted to say go on without him. He wanted to tell Tex how silly it was to eat while Angela was missing. But he didn't.

"Let me drop these manuals off in my room and I'll meet you and Liz in the hotel restaurant." Chris scooped up all the manuals. He planned to read them from start to finish after dinner so he wouldn't have trouble using the new equipment.

"Chris . . . I know how hard it must be for you to take time to eat while you could be studying how to use the new equipment or out there looking for Angela, but you've got to have strength to do what you must. That means you take time to eat and sleep. For Angela."

Chris silently thanked God for friends, but could only nod. He grabbed the sign that said, "außer Betrieb," and taped it to the back of the minibus.

***

"Emma. Are you okay?" Angela moved toward her as the door closed, confining them both in the locked area.

Emma had tears in her eyes and her shoulders sagged more than when Angela had last seen her. "I don't know. It's the same thing, every day. They keep asking questions about my family. I know what they're doing. They're trying to find out enough information about me to demand a ransom for my freedom."

Angela looked into Emma's eyes. "Everyone knows the US government won't pay a ransom. You hear it repeatedly on the news. They say paying kidnappers only causes more kidnappings. But, what about *me*? Couldn't the president make an exception for me?" She paused and looked into Angela's eyes. "My mother doesn't have any money. And, Daddy could care less what happens to me. I'll never get out of here."

"Did the kidnappers say they'd talked to your parents?"

Emma sniffed and dabbed at her eyes with her sleeve. "No. But only because they don't know who my parents are yet. These people will keep after me until I break. I know they will. And, God knows, I'm close to giving them what they want now."

"Did they cause you physical pain?"

"No. But I think they would if they felt it would help their cause. What happened to you when they took you this morning?" Emma looked concerned.

"Nothing. They tried to get me to wear a hijab."

Emma relaxed. "That's what they did to me the first day. I've still got a couple of them around here somewhere. I guess they gave up on forcing me to wear one."

"I was afraid they wanted my head covered to take me out on the streets," Angela said. "Have they ever taken you anywhere?"

"No." Emma didn't take time to think about it. "I've been right here the whole time."

"What about food and water?"

"Oh, I should have told you. We get sandwiches and bottles of water brought in every so often. It's not much, but it keeps the hunger pangs away for a while." Emma looked around. "There should be some here now."

Angela pointed to the food. "It's here, but I was afraid it might contain knockout drugs."

Emma raised her eyebrows. "Goodness. I didn't think of that. I've been eating the sandwiches and drinking the water since I got here five or so days ago."

"And you've not had any problems?"

"Other than crying more than usual? No, not really."

Angela grabbed one of the sandwiches and opened it. "I'll test this." She smiled.

Emma smiled back. "Okay. I'll test the water." She took the water bottle and unscrewed the cap.

It was the first time Angela had seen the young opera singer smile. She was beautiful. Angela prayed for Emma's safe release.

***

Chris dropped the operating manuals in his room and raced to the lobby on his way to the restaurant. A man approached him.

"*Entschuldigen Sie.* Uhh, . . . excuse me." He looked at a small piece of paper he was holding. "Are you not

Chris McCowan?"

The man's accent sent apprehension flooding over Chris. Then he remembered. A German translator was to find him at the hotel. "I'm Chris McCowan. And, you?"

"Heinz Gabriel. I am your translator." He extended his hand.

Chris took it and received a warm handshake. "I'm on my way to meet the others at the hotel restaurant. Would you like to join us?"

He smiled. "Yes. Naturally."

When they approached the table, Liz stood and Tex twirled his chair around.

"This is our translator, Heinz Gabriel. Heinz, this is . . . "

"Yes. I know," Heinz said before Chris could complete the introductions. He moved toward Liz. "You are Liz, of course."

She gave him one of her best hugs and a special smile.

He laughed as they separated. "They told me you are 'the hugger.' I didn't know what that meant until now. I was thinking 'tree hugger.' I've learned something new."

Liz pretended be surprised. "Who called me a hugger?"

"Everyone," Tex said before Heinz had a chance to answer.

They all laughed.

Tex continued. "I'm not complaining, mind you. I owe my sanity—my life actually—to Liz's hugs." When we met, I lived on the streets, and was drunk most of the time. Then, one day Liz hugged me. It didn't matter that my clothes smelled like I'd been living in them for a month—because I had. She didn't care about the body odor I'd gotten accustomed to that drove everyone else away. She looked me in the eye with her arms out and walked up and gave me the biggest ol' bear hug I'd ever had. It was the first human contact I'd had in months."

Liz's eyes glistened from the beginning of tears. "I guess I *am* a hugger."

Tex hugged her. "And she hugged me every time she saw me after that. She hugged me right off the street, into school, and into a job. I never had another drink after that first hug." Liz and Tex locked eyes for a time.

Heinz zeroed in on Tex. "You must be Tex. It's easy to tell who you are." He nodded toward the wheelchair. "And I wouldn't have said so, in the way I did, if they hadn't told me you are okay with your wheels."

Liz piped up. "Yeah, he's okay. It's the rest of us who have to suffer."

Chris laughed with Liz. "That leaves me. I don't want to hear what they told you about me. Whatever they said, it's all true."

Heinz looked at Chris and paused. "I know you're hurting and I can understand why. Use me to help any way I can. Not only translations, but whatever is needed."

Chris looked into Heinz's eyes, wondering how

much he could do to help find Angela. "I will. Thank you."

After they were seated, Liz turned to Heinz. "What I need help with right now is how to read this menu."

Heinz opened his own menu. "I can translate the main entrees for you, or you can tell me what you'd like and I'll order for you. Or, if we really want to simplify things, we can ask for English menus."

Tex looked at Liz with raised eyebrows. "English menus? Why didn't we think of that?"

**

Later, as they were eating, Tex asked about Heinz's background and how the man was selected to join their search for Angela.

"I am what you Americans call a corporate investigator, available by contract."

"You mean, like a private detective for corporations?" Tex asked.

"I think so. Private in the sense that I work on a contract basis for a limited time. However, I've been associated with the same company for several years."

"Brian's friends, I take it," Tex said.

A frown came over Heinz, then quickly disappeared. He nodded. "Yes, of course."

"What do you do for the company?" Chris forked a chunk of meat off the pork hock that covered his plate. He wanted to know how the Vengeance Squad could use Heinz for more than an interpreter.

Heinz finished chewing, swallowed, and laid his

fork on his plate. "Many things."

"For example?" Chris pressed. He wanted to know who he would be working with.

"Sometimes routine investigations. I might be asked to investigate a company my employers plan to work with. I check their financials, but then I go a little deeper. I talk to their associates, their suppliers, their competitors, even their employees."

Liz joined in. "Interesting. You do all that without letting them know who you're working for?"

"Naturally. I want to see the true picture, not the one the company wants me to see."

Chris pushed on. "Like corporate espionage?"

"Corporate spy?" Liz asked.

Heinz wiped his face with a napkin. "No. I am not a corporate spy. That is different. I am not saying it is not done. I have done it myself. The pay is good for such work. Still it can be boring and it takes much longer than a routine investigation."

"Just so you know," Chris said, "this group is made up of people with high morals, but . . . "

"That is good to hear." Heinz sipped his water.

"But, wait, I'm not finished. We have on occasion broken laws as long as no one was harmed in any way."

"Yes," Liz said. "Remember that time I told the hotel clerk my sister hadn't answered her phone and got him to give me a key to her room?" She looked at Heinz. "I don't have a sister."

"Yes," Chris said. "That's an example. But, I've done worse by transferring money from one bank to another."

Tex spoke up. "But only because the money had been stolen in the first place."

Chris looked at Heinz. "We stretch the laws sometimes but only when required to achieve a worthwhile goal. And we never hurt anyone except in self-defense. However, if we get caught we could be arrested. Even go to jail. Is this a group you want to work with?"

Heinz smiled. "Now I know what is meant by Vengeance Squad. I have heard what you did in America and in England. Nothing I learned causes me concern. I believe I can make it easier for you to do what must be done."

Chris straightened his knife and fork to make them parallel and then pushed back from his seat. "Good. Now, it's time to get to work and find my wife."

CHAPTER SEVEN

Back in his room after dinner, Chris picked up the first operations manual in the stack he'd brought from the minibus and started reading. For him, reading was the same as memorizing. Later, he would teach Tex how to get the most from their new toys.

Liz refused to learn anything related to technology. Michael had studied the technology and suggested the reader and the drone be combined. That way they could fly the reader around a wider area to find the RFID chip.

The larger drones were Phantom 4s with a flight time of twenty-eight minutes and the ability to take videos. If the camera was removed, he wondered, could it be replaced with the RFID reader? If not, could the RFID reader be redesigned to fit on the drone?

The idea for converting the drone continued to bug him after he went to bed. After a sleepless hour of tossing and turning he gave up trying to sleep, got dressed, and went to the minibus.

When he got there he found Heinz standing near the minibus, looking in a window. "Heinz? What are you doing here?"

Heinz looked surprised, but he quickly recovered. "I was out for a walk and saw this fine vehicle. It made me want to stop and look."

"This is our vehicle. They didn't tell you about it?"

Heinz paused. It was as if he was searching his brain for the right answer. "Oh, yes. They said something about an unusual bus, but I didn't know what that meant. So, this is for our use?"

"Yes. It's a bookmobile."

"Ah, we call it mobile library."

"This one is a library on one end and a control center on the other. We'll get together tomorrow and look it over and learn what all we have here."

"It is a fine vehicle." Heinz yawned. "I will see you in the morning. I go to sleep now."

Chris felt Heinz's reaction was strange. He watched as the translator departed and wondered what was going on. He shrugged. He'd worry about it later. Right now, he had an idea to test.

Based on the report Chris had seen in the FBI and MI6 files, Angela had been abducted by men who appeared to be Middle Eastern. No one had heard from her since. Was she still in the area? He didn't know. What he did know was that the only way to find her was by locating the RFID chip she wore.

He searched the boxes until he found one containing a large drone and another holding the RFID reader. He called Michael and coordinated with him while he fiddled with each one until they determined how to combine them. Satisfied, he locked the minibus and headed back to the hotel.

***

The next morning, the squad plus Heinz, met in Chris's room to discuss plans for the day. He looked at his friends and paused, beginning in the same way he did when he taught college courses. "I woke early this morning to see if MI6 had posted anything new about Angela's disappearance."

Heinz looked at him curiously. "They let you do that?"

Tex laughed. "Let's just say Chris is a wizard with computers."

"I see." Heinz nodded. "What did you learn?"

"That they're still searching for her. The only thing new was a verification of where the kidnapping happened, plus more details about the van that abducted her. In conjunction with the local law enforcement and traffic webcams, the agency has determined that the van didn't leave the neighborhood. It's not visible anywhere, so it must be inside a building."

"Can't they just search every building?" Tex asked.

"That would take forever," Heinz said. "The

refugee camp where she was taken is housed in an old airport. There are hundreds of abandoned buildings in and around the area."

Liz combed her gray hair back with her fingers. "Surely, Angela's friends are out there looking for that van around the clock."

Chris nodded. "They are, but like Heinz said, it's a large area to search. The report I read mentioned the region surrounding the camp is like a ghost town."

"That means the searchers probably aren't getting help from residents," Tex said.

"Right," Liz said. "Since there aren't any."

Chris held up a map of the area. "This is the only printed map I could find, and it's not the best for what we want to do. We'll use Google maps when we need more detail. This one will work for what I want to tell you today."

He paused and looked at each one before continuing. "I've marked the section on the map that MI6 identified as the best place to search. I didn't find information regarding their resources, number of people and type of equipment, but you can see it would take many people to cover an area this size in a reasonable amount of time—especially if they do so without alerting the kidnappers. There's no telling what would happen to the hostages if their captors felt threatened."

Heinz stood to get a closer look at the map. "You said *hostages*. Are there more than one?"

Chris bit his lip and took a deep breath. "Yes. Based on the reports I've read, there is at least one other person missing in the area."

"Who?" Liz asked.

"A twenty-one-year-old American opera singer who was doing volunteer work helping the refugees. Her name is Emma McCleary. She lives in Lübeck, Germany and performs regularly at the opera theater there. I checked their website and she's scheduled to sing Hirte in *Tosca* this weekend."

"Goodness," Liz said. "I wonder why she was kidnapped."

"Some Germans at the theater asked her to help here in Berlin on her day off and she volunteered. It's on her social network pages."

Liz shook her head. "She was trying to do a good thing and now she's missing. Did the report say she might be with Angela?"

"No, there was no connection discussed. But I hope they're together. Angela will help her."

"What about the FBI?" Tex asked. "Since this singer is American, is the FBI getting involved?"

"Yes." Chris pulled his laptop closer. "The FBI usually works only in the US, but they will go anywhere to help American citizens kidnapped in other countries. I cross-referenced some of the MI6 information with the FBI's data and learned the FBI dispatched an International Response Team to Berlin. The FBI agents were told to work with MI6 in the area near the Tempelhof Airport refugee camp." Chris looked at the screen of his laptop. "They should be here tomorrow."

"Wow," Liz said, "it's going to get crowded around

here."

"That brings up a point," Heinz said. "Will we be coordinating our efforts with UK and the US officials?"

Chris shook his head. "No. If they learn we're here, we'll be told to leave. They consider us amateurs and more trouble than help. We must do our job without being noticed. One thing we can be thankful for is that we'll have more freedom to act than they do. Their efforts may be restricted by protocols with Germany."

Tex rolled in closer to Chris. "In other words, we can get more done without them."

Chris nodded. "This map shows we have a difficult task ahead. I think the only approach is to come up with a way to reduce the search and we can only do that by coming up with unique ways of doing things.

"I called Michael and talked about it. He suggested we convert one of the large drones into a portable RFID reader. That'll let us scan the area faster and get into places we couldn't otherwise."

"Good idea," Tex said.

Liz smiled. "Michael is so smart. And you must have been up all night working that out with him. Are you okay?"

"I'm fine," Chris said. "It's kind of hard to sleep with Angela missing."

Liz cleared her voice. "I talked to Samuel last night and all is well in Hemington. I know we don't expect problems there, but we decided to keep in touch daily, just in case."

"Yes," Chris said. "MI6 might send someone there

to check on me, perhaps to tell me about Angela." He paused. "Actually, I'm pretty sure they know we're here." He looked around the room, stopping with Heinz for longer than he meant to. "Still, let me know if Samuel sees or hears anything out of the ordinary. We could make a list of questions he might be asked by MI6 . . . along with answers."

Everyone stared at Chris.

Liz broke the silence. "Or, we could let Samuel figure it out. He's British, you know."

Tex agreed. "Besides, we don't have time to prepare the Q and A. Our priority today should be finding and rescuing Angela."

Chris nodded, thankful for his friends to keep him on target. "Okay. Let's meet at the minibus. I think it'd be best if we spread out and don't appear to be together. I'll go first. Can I wear your Stetson, Tex? In case someone is watching."

"Sure. I'll wear a bandana. I wish I'd brought some costumes."

Chris nodded. "We'll buy more if we find a need. Heinz, why don't you walk with Liz."

"Naturally. I want to ask her about Samuel."

"Good. Tex, wait about ten minutes after I leave. Heinz and Liz, you two go about ten minutes after Tex."

***

Angela woke suddenly and, after remembering where she was, realized she'd been dreaming about Chris. She was on the floor close to where she and Emma had eaten sandwiches. She wondered if the food or water had made her drowsy, but decided not. Her mind was clearer now. She'd probably needed to rest. She'd been on high alert for . . . how long? She couldn't remember.

"Get off me, you pervert!" Emma spoke louder than Angela had heard her before.

Angela stood, moved cautiously toward the young woman's voice, thinking briefly about her plan not to give away her strength and training. A fraction of a second later she had a man in a choke hold and constrained herself from putting him to sleep forever. Instead, she threw him to the floor and stomped on him with her foot.

The young opera singer stood, then moved away from the man, shaky and in tears. "Thank you. That sicko climbed on me while I was sleeping. What kind of person does that?"

Angela got into a defensive stance and waited for him to retaliate.

He didn't go after her, though. Instead he stared at her much too long and then screamed. "You fake."

His loud, broken English told her he knew she could have killed him. And he now knew she was trained to fight.

It was too bad, but she'd had to get him away from Emma. Perhaps she could have taken more of a civilian-like action to reach the same result, but it was too late to consider that now. She'd lost the advantage of surprise if there were more encounters.

Nizar came into the room, pistol raised. He'd

probably heard Sayid's scream. Angela noted the time it took for Nizar to respond.

Sayid, still on the floor rubbing his neck, spoke in Arabic. "Shoot her. She is enemy soldier."

Nizar sized up the situation and laughed. "You let this girl beat you? Don't be scared. I will protect you."

"Shoot her." Sayid's eyes bulged and his face turned red. "Shoot or I'll shoot you when I get my gun."

"We can't shoot her. We must take her to Reyaad Amin." Nizar waved a hand toward Emma and Angela. "Leave women alone. Amin will not like it if you damage the goods."

The name Amin shocked Angela so much she feared they could see it on her face. She closed her mouth and walked toward Emma, comforting her and pretending to ignore their conversation. They may have learned she could hold her own in hand-to-hand combat, but she hadn't shown she understood Arabic.

Reyaad Amin was the most successful ISIS recruiter in all the refugee camps, the target of her investigation. The man responsible for increasing the number of enemy soldiers on the battlefield was within her reach.

"Come." Nizar beckoned Sayid. "We must tell Reyaad about the strong one. He'll know what to do."

Angela watched them as they moved toward the door then put her arms around Emma who sobbed.

"No!" It was Sayid's voice.

Emma screamed.

Angela turned to see Sayid racing toward her with

a knife in his hand. She pushed Emma away, grabbed the arm with the weapon, and twisted it until he fell to the floor, dropping the knife as he landed. She took the weapon and moved toward him with the knife pointing toward his belly. She'd had enough of this character.

The sound of a gunshot kept her from slicing Sayid open. "Stop." Nizar spoke English.

Angela looked up to see Nizar's gun pointed at her. If he was crazy enough to put a hole in the ceiling, he might shoot her for the fun of it.

His eyes narrowed and he was all seriousness. For a few seconds. Then he laughed and lowered the gun. "Get up, fool," he said in Arabic to Sayid who appeared to be in shock.

He couldn't get up though. Angela still held the knife near his stomach, wishing she could slice him open.

***

When Tex and Chris got to the control room, Tex pulled the bandana off his head and grabbed his Stetson from Chris. "I felt absolutely naked out there without my hat. Remind me to get you a costume if you want to hide from MI6."

Chris laughed. "I thought you looked good in that red bandana. Reminded me of Willie Nelson."

Heinz and Liz climbed into the control room. "*Guten Morgen*," Liz said.

"Learned a little German, did you?"

Liz smiled. "Very little. Good morning is simple. You should have seen us. Heinz spoke German and I acted like I understood. If anyone was watching they would have sworn we were having a conversation. I have no idea what he said, though."

Heinz laughed. "It was all nice, dear lady."

Tex rolled around the desk. "All I got to do was wear a bandana. Big deal. Tomorrow I'm bringing my makeup and all my costumes. Chris wore my Stetson. Stretched it out, I bet."

Liz hugged Tex. "Don't be silly. How could he? Your head is bigger than his."

Tex smiled and picked up one of the boxes. "We need to know how these *Wireless IFB Inductive Earpieces* work before we go anywhere. What does IFB stand for?"

Everyone shrugged except Chris who had read every word of the instruction manual and had looked up the acronym on the internet. "IFB is short for interrupted fold back or interruptible feedback. It's an earpiece that on-air personnel wear to get instructions from their producers. The technology is difficult to explain, but let's say it allows staff to talk to the news readers without feedback and noise."

Liz opened the box to expose a flesh-colored object designed to go in a person's ear. "Why do *we* need them?"

Chris answered. "I thought this would be the best way to communicate without everyone on the street knowing what we were doing. We'll need to wear a neck loop for it to work, but the loop can be worn under our clothes."

Liz picked up one of the earpieces and examined it. "Yuk. I don't want one of these things in my ear." She stuck it in anyway. "Hmm, doesn't feel bad. Somebody say something."

Tex picked up an earpiece and put it in his ear. "Hello, Liz. Can you hear me?"

"Well, of course I can hear you. I'm sitting next to you, for goodness' sakes."

Tex rolled to the far corner and whispered, "Can you hear me now?"

Liz smiled. "Yes. Much better. I can hear you through the earpiece."

Tex rolled back to the desk. "Good. So, what's on the agenda for today?"

"Liz, I'd like you to get familiar with the bookmobile this morning. And, before you ask, yes, you need to wear the earpiece and neck loop in case we need to talk to you privately if there is a patron in there with you."

Tex spun his wheelchair around to face Chris. "What about me?"

"Tex, I'd like you and Heinz to check out the neighborhood to get the lay of the land. Perhaps you can pretend to be an invalid and Heinz is your caregiver pushing you around the area. You'll both need earpieces and neck loops."

Tex pushed his Stetson back and showed his best grin. "You mean the way we did in Albuquerque that time. I was the elderly rich guy and you were my servant."

"Something like that." Chris smiled thinking about the trip to New Mexico with Tex. "Don't get carried away playing the part. That'll make you more noticeable."

"Will the minibus be here when we get back?" Heinz asked.

"No. We'll move to the spot where Angela was kidnapped. Over by the old Tempelhof Airport."

"What about the pistols?" Tex raised his eyebrows and looked hopeful. "Should I take my gun?"

Liz made a funny sound. "Naaa. You don't need a gun."

Chris nodded. "Liz is right. Let's leave them in the storage space behind the driver's seat. We can also put the drones and other equipment there. The operations control section is nice, but it doesn't have much in the way of storage space."

Tex looked disappointed. "What if I need a gun while we're out looking around?"

"You won't. All I want you to do today is to get familiar with the area. Check out the buildings, the people, the traffic. Later, if we have a need to go after people, we'll talk about taking the guns."

It hadn't been long since Tex's presidential pardon allowed him to carry arms again. Back home anyway. Not here. Chris didn't know what the law was here, but he suspected it wouldn't allow foreigners to carry weapons.

Liz turned to Heinz. "Before you go, could you pick out some books and magazines the refugees might like? Looks like all we have in the bookmobile is

German-language books. Wouldn't it be best to have something in Arabic?"

"I'll see what I can do." Heinz tapped his temple as if he was making a note.

"Okay, everyone," Chris said, "let's get started. I'll drive. Heinz, will you ride up front to help me with the road signs?"

CHAPTER EIGHT

Nizar's warning didn't stop Angela. She lifted the knife gently to where the point touched Sayid's stomach. If anyone moved, or she shifted her weight, the blade could enter him quickly.

Nizar fired again and she saw residue from the impact of the bullet close to where Emma cowered. Angela stood and tossed the knife. It rattled as it hit the tiled floor.

Sayid crouched, moved away from Angela, got to his feet when he got close to Nizar.

"See, she is crazy," Sayid spoke Arabic.

"And you are a baby," Nizar said.

Sayid reached for the gun in Nizar's hand. "She must die."

Nizar lifted the gun and brought it down hard

against Sayid's jaw. The force was enough to knock the man to his knees. He looked up, pleading, as blood dripped from his mouth.

"You fool," Nizar said. "Get up! Get out of here."

The rapid, violent attack surprised Angela. She tightened her already defensive stance.

Nizar followed Sayid out of the room, slamming the gun into his back when he seemed to resist.

When they were gone and the door closed, Angela turned to Emma. "Are you okay?"

Emma nodded slowly, tears in her eyes. "I guess. I'm not hurt. Just scared. Who *are* you?"

"That's not important. Stay with me and I'll do my best to protect you until we get out of here."

Emma's eyes opened wide. "Did my mother send you to rescue me?"

"I'm afraid not."

"It was Daddy?"

"No. To tell the truth I didn't know you'd been kidnapped until I met you here."

"So, no one is looking for me?"

"I wouldn't say that. Your friends saw you get kidnapped. I'm sure they've called the police and notified the American Embassy. Surely someone is looking for you right now."

Emma was quiet. Then she looked at Angela. "You can get us out, right?"

"I'm going to try. I'm sure there are people looking for me, too."

"I hope someone finds us soon."

"How many guards do they have here?" She didn't

think of them as guards, but Emma seemed to, so she called them that, too. In Angela's mind they were terrorists.

"I don't know." Emma pushed back and looked at Angela. "Should I be counting them? I don't understand."

"If you want to escape, we need to know what we're up against. I've counted four. How many different people have you seen?"

Emma counted on her fingers. "Five, I think."

"Okay, good. Let's compare which ones we know and see which one I'm missing. I've seen Sayid, Liliane, and Nizar. I've heard the name Reyaad Amin. What about you?"

"Oh, my goodness. I don't know any of their names. There's the woman, of course. Then the fat one who tried to rape me. The vulgar, ugly one who pointed the gun at you, and the nice one who always smiles at me. And, there's the boss they all refer to, but I haven't seen him."

"Hmm. I haven't met the nice one. Is he the one who took you away yesterday while I was gone?"

"Yes. That was the one."

Before they could finish counting the enemy, Sayid and Nizar returned. Sayid carried an electronic device Angela didn't recognize. He walked toward Angela. Nizar grabbed Emma and pulled her away

Angela kicked Sayid in the groin. He crumbled to the floor, the device he'd carried bouncing near him. Sayid screamed something Angela thought meant witch. She wasn't sure though. She hadn't learned the word in her Arabic training. He could have said something worse. She enjoyed his response. It made it worth what she knew was coming next.

They surprised her though. She expected some physical payback. Instead, Emma screamed. Angela turned and saw Nizar holding a knife to Emma's neck. The woman's scream ended, but her eyes bulged with fear.

In broken English, Nizar said to Angela, "You. Be still. Or I hurt this one."

Sayid was up on all fours. He groaned and moved into a crouch. Once he was on his feet, he moved toward Angela with hate in his eyes. She steadied herself and took a defensive stance.

Nizar told Sayid in Arabic to forget her and do what he was sent to do.

Sayid stared at Nizar long enough to make Angela wonder if he would disregard Nizar and come after her anyway. He didn't. He recovered his device and waved it over Angela's body, being careful not to get in position for her to kick him again. He ran it up one side of her and then the other. When the machine neared her back, it beeped.

He smiled, and said in Arabic, "Reyaad precise. She's wired. We were right to tell him she is soldier. We should get medals. Her friends will be looking for her. We have to get out of here before they find her."

Nizar nodded. "Yes. But, we can't take the thing that beeps. Leave it here so they'll think she is here."

"But it is under her clothes."

Nizar looked at Sayid. Paused. "Liliane! Come in

here."

Liliane came running in.

"You worthless woman," Nizar said. "You were supposed to search the prisoners." He nodded toward Angela. "This one has an electronic bug under her shirt in back. Her friends will be here soon to save her and kill us. Get that thing off her quickly. Leave it here."

He switched to English to address Angela. "This woman will take device. If you try to escape while we are out of the room, your friend there will die." He continued to hold the knife close to Emma's neck. "Do you understand?"

Angela nodded slowly, praying MI6 would rescue them soon.

The terrorists left the room with Emma who continued to sob.

Liliane removed Angela's shirt and told Angela to take off her bra. Liliane took the bra and tossed it on the floor. "Put the shirt back on," Liliane said as she handed it to Angela.

The woman pushed her toward the door. "We go now."

When Angela got to the other room, Nizar still had his knife out, but it was no longer near Emma's neck.

Angela watched for an opportunity to act. If it was only her, she could outrun these clowns. But she couldn't leave Emma alone. Emma would never survive.

They all walked through the room and out another door. Angela was surprised to see the van she'd been forced into when they had nabbed her. She didn't want to leave the building and the RFID chip. There was a better chance to be rescued if she stayed put.

Nizar must have noticed her reluctance because he moved the knife up to Emma's neck and motioned for Angela to lean against the side of the van. With Emma's safety jeopardized, Angela had to comply.

She soon knew why they wanted her to stand there. The device that had found the RFID chip was activated and moved back and forth across her back along the place where the chip used to be.

When Nizar was satisfied that Angela was no longer bugged, he pushed her into the van.

Angela said a quick prayer for Emma and for a way to let the agency know they were being moved. Nothing came to mind until she saw the driver, a man she hadn't met, wearing the wristwatch she'd had on when she'd been taken prisoner. Thank you, Lord.

***

Chris drove the minibus to a spot near the entrance to the refugee camp where Angela had last been seen. He found a parking place on the street near an abandoned building.

They closed the bookshelf door that separated the bookmobile section from the operations control area. Liz stayed in the bookmobile while Chris sat at|one of the computers.

Heinz manned the lift for Tex to exit the minibus. When they were on the pavement, ready to go look around, Chris called out the door. "Check your communications systems. Make sure we can all hear each other."

Tex responded first. "I can hear you in stereo."

"Can you hear me?" It was Liz.

"Yes," Heinz said. "I can."

"Okay," said Chris. "I hear everyone. Keep your systems on at all times. If I find something to indicate we need to move, it may happen quickly. Okay?"

"I understand," Tex said.

"Me, too," Heinz said.

"I'm already in the minibus," said Liz.

After Tex and Heinz left, Chris went over Michael's idea for combining the RFID reader and the drone and decided it should work.

The maximum distance for the reader was thirty feet. Because his only experience with the technology had been retail store use and toll road applications, he'd feared they'd have to get closer for the device to work.

Another bit of information he found from his research was that encryption efforts for chips had not blocked talented hackers. UK's encrypted passport chips were hacked in less than forty-eight hours after the chips were first introduced. If the encrypted data was that easy for an amateur to crack, he wouldn't have any problems doing it.

Once he had a better understanding of how the RFID technology worked, he hacked into the MI6 computers to search for Angela's radio frequency.

Before long, Chris was deep into cyberspace and excited about how fast the new computers got him there.

Then, he found it. The angel frequency, they called it, referring to Angela.

He pulled out the RFID readers and went to work. In a matter of seconds lights on one of the devices flashed red. The operating manual said that meant a signal was being received. Joy overcame him. Could he be so lucky? Was she only thirty feet away?

RFID chips could be read through minibus walls and buildings unlike technology such as barcodes. It excited him to think she could be so near. But, something was wrong. The signal he read didn't match the angel frequency. What he was seeing was some other RFID chip.

It was a disappointment, but his enthusiasm wasn't squelched because the RFID reader worked. After digging around in the box for more information, he found the test chip he'd discovered last night. It was still on. Sadly, he turned it off and the red flashing light went dark.

It wasn't Angela. Not yet. He'd have to get closer to find her.

*****

Angela hated to leave the vicinity without her RFID chip. She'd worn it, or one like it, for years, and never gave it a second thought. Without it, she was all alone.

But not totally. God was watching over her. And her wristwatch was in the same vehicle with her and she was thankful for that. Nathan was probably tracking it and wasn't far behind. She hoped. She also hoped the driver wearing her watch would stay nearby.

They'd tied her hands behind her with rope and made her sit in the back of the van where there were no windows. Emma was in the middle seat, crying, with Liliane on her right and Nizar on her left. Sayid was in front in the passenger seat. It wasn't long before Angela learned the driver's name was Volker. He appeared to be German and couldn't be the fifth guard Emma talked about, the nice one who smiled.

As usual, Angela continued to formulate escape scenarios. She wasn't being watched closely since there were no doors in the back of the van.

They weren't the smartest bad guys she'd ever run across. For one thing, they didn't know how to tie hands. She'd held her arms slightly apart as they tightened the knot so she could get loose when she wanted to. But she needed a plan first.

What would she do if she freed her hands? She could overpower Liliane and go out the other woman's door at a traffic stop. What then? Nizar had a gun.

That was a deterrent, especially since he was sitting next to Emma. That was the main problem. Emma. Any escape plan Angela came up with would have to include taking Emma with her. Emma would never make it on her own.

All Angela could do was figure out where they were going. If she got the chance to call for help, she'd need to know where she was. She looked out the front windshield to watch for landmarks and memorized streets they crossed.

Until Nizar caught her. "I see what you are doing," he said softly in English. "Turn around and shut your eyes or I will blindfold you. Is that what you want?"

Emma whimpered. "Please! Let me go home. I won't tell anyone. Please. Please."

Liliane and Nizar snickered.

Liliane shushed Emma as if she was a child. But, both Liliane and Nizar were quieter than usual. It was as if they were concerned about what the front seat might hear. Did that mean the driver, the German, wasn't aware of what was going on?

Angela turned and didn't look up, but she continued to memorize the route, approximating distances and noting turns, even short stops caused by traffic lights or congestion.

Before long the route became so intricate she was afraid all the effort had been in vain. She'd never be able to tell anyone where she'd been taken, even if she had an opportunity. But, soon her prayers were answered once again.

Sayid and the driver openly discussed the best way to get to the Syrian Refugee Camp in Mitte, a borough in Berlin. They spoke in Arabic, unaware of Angela's ability to understand them. She had studied all the camps in Germany before going to the Tempelhof Airport location. She knew exactly where they were taking her. Maybe she'd get to meet Amin there.

CHAPTER NINE

Something about the RFID test chip bugged Chris. He turned it on and off several times while his brain worked. Soon, he had the solution, an improvement to what Michael had suggested.

He pulled the microphone in close. "Attention everyone. Please return to the control center."

Liz pushed open the door from the bookmobile. "What'd you find? Did you get a signal for Angela?"

Chris pulled out the drone. "Not exactly. Wait until Tex and Heinz get here so I can tell everyone at once."

When the guys arrived, Chris waited while Tex used the lift to enter the control center.

"What's up?" Tex asked. "Did you find Angela's location?"

Chris held up the drone. "No, but I have an idea how we can find her."

"Tell us," Heinz said.

Chris placed the drone on the desk next to the RFID reader. "Remember Michael's idea I told you about? Of replacing the drone camera with an RFID reader?"

"Yeah," Liz said. "Sounded like a good idea to me."

"Doing that would let us move the chip reader in closer," Tex said. "And, it would also let us cover more area faster."

"Yes," Chris said, "but we'd be flying blind. Here's all we have to do." Chris picked up the drone, taped the reader to the bottom of the drone with duct tape, then turned the reader and the drone on. He watched Tex to see if he figured it out.

"Looky there," Tex said, pointing to the computer screen. "We can watch the reader to see if it finds something. I assume the light will blink, right?"

"Yes. Here is a test chip." Chris turned on the test chip and the light flashed on the reader as well as the computer screen.

Heinz nodded slowly. "Ah ha. I see. We fly that machine around until it finds the chip. You know how to fly a drone like this?"

"Chris flew one in England when we were there on a case," Tex said. "But that was a homemade job. This one is probably more sophisticated."

"I know where is a park," Heinz said. "Is good place to practice. Won't attract attention there."

Chris stood. "Good idea. Let's do it."

Heinz handed a shopping bag to Liz. "Before we go, I must give you this. These are books you wanted. In Arabic. A variety of books, some for children and some for adults."

Liz gave him a hug. "Well, aren't you sweet. That's perfect. We'll be ready if refugees stop by. How much do I owe you?"

Heinz put out both hands. "Oh, no. I pay. My gift to you."

***

Chris had memorized the operating manual, but flying the drone in an open field was the best way to become proficient.

Heinz was right. Chris needed to practice flying the machine, and the park was an ideal place for it. He hoped it wouldn't take long, as he detested every moment that kept him from actively searching for Angela.

All he had to do was learn enough to fly it to where Angela might be without crashing it. He was sure she was somewhere near and that they would find her soon.

At the park, he placed the drone on a picnic table along with the plane's remote control unit and a digital tablet to show what the drone saw in real time.

They checked the duct tape holding the RFID reader on the drone and positioned the reader so its light would show without blocking the rest of the drone's view. If they got a hit, they'd need to see where it was.

When they were ready, Heinz held the drone and stepped off twenty feet. With the remote control, Chris flew the drone out of Heinz's hands. The control unit had two toggle switches, each controlled two of the four propellers.

Once in the air, Chris made small moves at a low altitude until he gained enough confidence to make the drone soar.

Tex rolled up closer to Chris. "Hey, that looks like fun. Let me try it."

"Next time, Tex. I want to get this baby out searching for Angela as quickly as possible."

Tex pouted, but he didn't ask again.

Heinz helped explain, his eyes locked on Tex's. "Looks like Chris can fly the drone and find Angela. Maybe it is best we do that now. When she's home safe, we can all play with the drone. Okay?"

Tex squinted at Heinz. "Yeah. I knew Chris could learn in a hurry. He made his own drone last time, back before you could buy them everywhere."

Chris landed the drone at their feet and turned off the controller. "Yes, but this is different. Visually, it feels like I'm on the drone. I like that. That means I can fly to someplace and look around, places I wouldn't be able to see otherwise."

"It looks like you were doing just fine," Liz said.

Chris loved having Liz around. She was always positive. Nothing rattled her unless it was serious. "Okay. I'm ready. Any ideas where we should start looking?"

Tex swiveled his chair, pointed himself toward the minibus. "Heinz and I spotted a building not far from here that would be an ideal hideout for someone wanting to stay in the shadows. Looks like an old beer garden. Windows are boarded up. There's a garage door where a van could have entered to hide from MI6. Plus, it's close to where Angela was last seen. It was locked up tight, unlike some of the dilapidated buildings around here that anyone could get into."

Chris picked up the drone and carried it and the controller to the minibus. "Sounds perfect. Take me there."

Tex rolled along with him. "Aren't you afraid we might spook them?"

"Hmm. You might be right. Let's go back to where we were and we can fly this baby from there."

When they got there, Tex suggested Heinz show Chris the suspicious-looking building. "Why don't you go with Chris and show him the building we found. That way we'll draw less attention to ourselves."

"Good idea," Chris said. "Then I'll come back here to fly the drone and Heinz can stay there to spot for me."

***

When Chris returned from viewing the target building, he placed the drone on the pavement outside the minibus, turned the machine on, and pushed both throttles to allow it to soar into the air. He let it hover there while he climbed inside the minibus and placed the controller on the desk.

"From here, I'll go by what's shown on the digital tablet screen. Since I'm going to be busy flying and making sure I don't smash into any buildings, I want someone to watch for the RFID reader to light up."

Tex rolled in closer. "I'll do that."

Liz moved in, too. "Me, too. Won't hurt to have four eyes watching."

"Good." Chris adjusted the speed and aimed toward where he hoped the target building was. "Heinz? Let us know when you see the drone."

"Will do." Heinz's voice came into Chris's ear loud and clear.

"Look," said Chris, "that's the building." He turned the drone's camera to face backward and down. "And there's Heinz. Can you see the drone, Heinz?"

Heinz waved toward the drone. "Sure can."

"He's waving at us," Tex said.

Chris wiped his hands on his shirt and got fresh grips on the drone controls. "Now's the time to watch for the red light to flash on the RFID reader. I'm going to fly slowly from one end of the building to the other as well as over the top."

"What's that?" Tex pointed at the display of what the drone could see.

Chris stared at the screen and saw what looked like something flapping on the screen. "I don't know. It wasn't there a minute ago."

Liz turned to Chris. "Did the reader come loose? I was looking at the place where the red light should be and suddenly it moved sideways."

Chris set the drone to hover so he could study the display. "You know what? I think a piece of duct tape holding the RFID reader came off. The tape probably worked loose from the motion and vibrations of the drone motors. The red light is still visible, but . . . should we abort and secure the reader to the drone? I'd hate for it to fall off and be lost on the roof of that building. We don't have another one like it."

Chris turned the drone for the trip back. "Heinz, we're seeing something that indicates the duct tape is coming loose. Can you see it? Are we right? Should we abort to keep from losing the reader?"

"Wait," Tex said. "Stop. The red light is flashing. We've found something."

"I see it, too," Liz said.

Then Chris saw it. He felt relieved, knowing it might mean they'd found Angela. "Heinz, never mind the duct tape. Can you still see the drone?"

"Yes. And I saw the red light flash, too. I can tell you exactly where it happened. Do you want to land the drone? I can take it back to the minibus."

"Yes," Chris said. "That'll save me from flying over the buildings again and prevent the RFID reader from falling off and getting lost."

Heinz spoke softer. "Be cautious. There is a new vehicle parked about a block away."

"Thanks. Did everyone hear that? Let's all be careful."

***

Sayid and the driver continued to discuss the route in German, making it unnecessary for Angela to track the van's progress mentally. She no longer had to sneak peeks out the front window, eliminating Nizar's need to threaten her.

She pretended to be asleep so they wouldn't know she was listening. She tried to remember what she'd been taught about the Mitte Camp during training in London.

Although the intelligence reports had emphasized the Tempelhof Airport camp where Amin had been seen, part of her preparation was to study other refugee camps in Germany and to select the camps that would most likely attract ISIS recruiters.

When Germany's Chancellor Ranke adopted an open-door policy toward refugees fleeing Syria and other war-torn countries, the response exceeded Germany's ability to vet and care for those who poured in. Other EU countries set limits to how many they would accept, forcing more to go to Germany.

During the orientation classes, Angela learned there were German refugee camps in Mannheim, Munich, and Holzdorf. In Berlin, camps were set up in Charlottenburg, Mitte, Kreuzberg, Neukölln, and Tempelhof Airport.

MI6 sent her and Nathan to the Tempelhof location to find ISIS recruiters since it was the largest refugee camp in the country. That turned out to be a good choice, except that she was now a prisoner.

The Mitte camp, where they were going now, was much smaller. She wondered where the kidnappers would hide her and Emma. Were they stopping for Amin and then going elsewhere?

Angela thought of the driver wearing her watch, and wondered whether he'd stay close enough for Nathan to track them.

****

When Heinz got back to the minibus with the modified drone he joined the others in the operations control section. Chris pocketed the RFID reader and put the drone in its storage box. He grabbed a couple of beetle drones from the drawer and put them in his coat pocket.

He looked at Heinz. "Tell us about that car you saw near the building."

"It was strange to see the auto pull in slowly and park the way it did. Odder still when no one got out. It may not mean anything since we are not aware of the usual routine here. But in a place where there are not many vehicles, this one stood out."

"Was the car close enough for someone inside to see the drone?" Tex asked.

Heinz nodded. "Yes."

Chris pulled on the end of his beard. "We have to assume someone is watching."

"It's probably MI6," Liz said. "Let them watch. Maybe they'll help."

"MI6 would help us," Heinz said. "We are all looking for Angela."

"Or, they might send us home," Chris said. "I don't

want to take a chance on that happening. They've had ample time to work with us and they haven't returned my calls."

Heinz nodded. "I see."

Chris continued. "We need to get into that building where we got the hit on the RFID reader. And we need to do so now. I don't care who sees us, but I don't want MI6 hindering our investigation and I don't want the local police to arrest us for breaking and entering."

Tex took off his Stetson and rubbed his forehead. "What's the plan?"

Chris pulled one of the beetles out of his pocket and held it up for all to see. "The plan is to fly this into the building where we think the RFID is located and look around. If it appears safe, we'll go in."

"What about the camera with the flexible lens?" Tex said. "We can look in the building with that, too. All we need is a cracked window or some space under a door."

"Good idea," Chris said. "Get a couple of them to take along."

Tex opened the drawer behind the driver's seat and looked in for the cameras. "This might be a good time to take the guns."

Chris nodded. "Yes, if the reader is correct and Angela is there, we may need weapons to free her." He looked at Tex. "Get them, but keep them hidden unless we have to use them."

"Please," Liz said, "don't shoot anybody."

Tex handed Chris the Glock and put the .45 in the

pack on the back of the wheelchair. "We won't. Not unless it's necessary."

"Got an extra weapon for me?" Heinz asked.

Chris looked at Heinz for several seconds, considering his question. "No. Afraid not. Only have these two."

He clipped the holster and gun on his belt under his coat. "Liz, I'd like you to stay here and watch the minibus . . . ."

"I'm not hanging around here while y'all go find Angela. We can lock the minibus, you know."

"Liz, I just want you to be safe . . . ."

"Don't you worry about me. I've been shot at more'n once and I'm still living. I'll do my part. Just tell me what it is."

"I go with Miss Liz," Heinz said.

Chris nodded. "Good. Okay, here's the plan. Tex will take a position to the west of the entry to the building Heinz will point out. Heinz, you take Liz with you to the east side of the door. Don't go far. I'll send a beetle to see if anyone is in there. Tex, use that flexible-lens camera to look around inside. Heinz, take a flexible lens camera for your end. Let me know if either of you see anything."

"What do we do after that?" Tex asked.

"It depends on what we find. If there's nobody outside watching, we find a way to get in the building. Angela might be tied up in an inner room and not visible with our equipment."

"And if someone is there?" Heinz asked.

"Depends. If we see Angela, we go in. If we don't,

we'll talk."

"Let's do it," Tex said.

"Make sure you have your earpiece in place and turned on. Tex, you go first. I'll go second. Heinz and Liz will bring up the rear. Heinz, you and Liz need to lock up this place before you leave."

CHAPTER TEN

Angela was awakened by the sound of a car horn. She was groggy, unsure where she was. It came to her quickly. They were on the way to the Mitte Refugee Camp. Must be close. Surely, she hadn't slept long.

Why had she slept at all? Had she been drugged again? Probably not. The power of suggestion from pretending to be asleep so she could covertly listen to Volker and Sayid talk in German was most likely the culprit. She couldn't remember when she'd had a good sleep.

The trip from one camp to the other would take thirty minutes or so based on her memory of discussing it in the class she attended prior to going to Germany. That meant she couldn't have slept long. She had to stay alert if she was going to get out of this alive.

The horn sounded again and the van swerved, causing her to slide to the right. She looked up, not caring what she'd been told. No one said anything this time. Everyone was looking out the front window to see the cause of the ruckus.

After a few more honks and turns, the van came to a halt.

"I told you to keep your head down." It was Nizar. "Do you want me to hurt this pretty young woman?" He had an all too friendly hold on Emma.

Angela glared at him. "No. I want you to let us go."

He laughed. "Can't do that." He tightened his hold on Emma. "We're here. Ready to see your new home?"

Angela saw a tall, barbed-wire fence through the windshield. As the kidnappers opened doors, not paying attention to her, she took it all in.

Would this be the place to make a run for it? Her hands were still tied behind her, but she could slip loose anytime she wanted. Doing so might be just the surprise needed to get away.

Nizar was on the pavement helping Emma out and pretending to bump into her as he did. The others saw him and laughed. Except for Volker. He seemed ashamed of his friends.

Nizar's gun was in his waistband. No holster, not even a belt. Angela could grab it as she exited. They were all looking at him and his attempts to paw Emma. The woman was fighting him off, causing them all to laugh more.

Angela went through the possibilities of outcomes if she wiggled her hands out of the rope and retrieved Nizar's gun. What then? The others were armed, no doubt, except maybe Liliane. And Emma was too close to Nizar to get away. Even if Angela got the gun, she couldn't get Emma free before one of the other captors fired.

This wasn't the time for escape.

***

Chris got the beetle into the building on the first try. He flew it around until he saw a man in a suit. At that point, Chris landed the beetle on the floor and turned it toward the man hoping he might lead Chris to Angela.

"Attention everyone," Chris looked down toward the communications loop hanging around his neck even though it was sensitive enough to pick up his voice with his head up. "There's a man in the building near me."

"What does he look like? Middle Eastern?"

"No. Neatly dressed, white, military posture."

"Is he armed?" Tex asked.

"I don't think so. Let me check." Chris looked at his phone which served as a monitor for images from the beetle drone. He turned the beetle a little to the right for a better view. "My display is small, but it looks like his hands are empty. That doesn't mean he doesn't have a weapon on him or nearby."

"What do you want to do?" Tex asked through the comm.

Chris didn't hesitate. "Angela could be there. I'm going in. Uh-oh, wait."

"What's wrong?" Tex's concern came through loud and clear.

"I think he's spotted the beetle. He's walking toward it with long strides." The screen went dark. "I was right. I can't see anything. He must have stepped on it. There's no sense in sending in another beetle. Someone bring me a flexible camera. I need to see what's going on. We must find Angela now."

Heinz got to Chris first. They slipped the lens under the door. They could see what was inside the door on Heinz's phone.

Liz and Tex joined them, the four of them outside the place where the RFID chip had been detected. Chris held a finger in front of his mouth, and whispered. "Someone inside is walking toward the door."

Heinz retracted the flexible lens and backed away from the door. Tex rolled his wheelchair into position about ten feet away. He reached around to his backpack and drew his pistol, and aimed it toward the door. Chris had his pistol out, too. He motioned for Heinz and Liz to move to the side.

The door opened and a man walked out as if he were going for a stroll. He stopped and stared at the gun in Tex's hand. Chris moved behind the man to keep him from going back in the building. Heinz moved in to block one escape route while Liz covered the other.

The man recovered from his initial shock, raised

his hands and grinned. "Whoa. Chris McCowan, I presume." He looked around, nodding. "And his merry band of avengers."

Chris kept the gun pointed at him. "Who are you?"

The man didn't answer Chris's question, but continued to talk. "I was told you might show up, but I had no idea who you had working with you." He looked around. "A cowboy dude in a wheelchair, an old granny, and—"

"Okay," Liz said. "I've changed my mind. You can shoot this one."

The man gulped and looked around in a way that said he didn't know if she was kidding. He held his hands up higher and looked at her with raised eyebrows.

"How do you know my name?" Chris tried a different tactic.

"The photo on Angela's desk gave you away, I'm afraid. Can I put my arms down now?"

"You saying you're Angela's partner?"

"Yes. Of course."

Heinz turned to Chris. "He sounds like he knows you and your wife."

Chris wasn't convinced. "Then he should tell us where she is."

"She's not here." The man started to lower his arms. And we're not going to find her arguing about who knows what."

"Check his ID," Liz said.

"Good idea." Chris moved to where he could get a clean shot if the man tried anything. "Go easy. Pull out your ID slowly."

The prisoner didn't move. "Sorry. We don't carry ID in the field. It's back in the hotel safe."

Chris remembered Angela had no ID when he first met her. Maybe this guy was telling the truth.

"I've got a phone," the man offered.

"Show me," Chris said. "Probably a burner phone."

"No. I have one of those, too, though. I brought my work phone today in case Angela called."

Chris nodded toward Tex. "Give the phones to the cowboy dude in the wheelchair. Slowly, carefully."

The man complied.

"I still don't know your name," Chris said.

"Nathan Marlowe." He lowered his arms, bowed slightly. "I'm surprised Angela never mentioned me."

"I don't like your silly grin," Liz said. "We're here to find Angela. Don't get in our way."

Chris didn't show it, but he was surprised to feel Liz's anger. She didn't show it often. Nathan, or whoever was, seemed to bring out that response, with his flippant answers to their questions.

Nathan's eyes narrowed. "Sorry, ma'am. Didn't mean to belittle the reason we're all here. We've worked day and night to find her and I'm afraid nerves are somewhat frayed."

Tex checked both phones while everyone waited. "He seems legit. The burner phone hasn't been used. His other phone has all kinds of stuff on it he shouldn't be carrying on the job. Facebook shows he's Nathan Marlowe, lives in London with Edith, two children and a dog. His birthday was last week. Turned thirty-two."

Nathan sputtered. "I told you I don't usually carry that phone. It should be in the hotel room safe along with my ID. I brought it to help find Angela."

Chris ignored him and looked toward Tex. "You satisfied he's legit?"

Tex nodded and stowed his weapon in his wheelchair back pack.

Chris holstered his weapon. "Were you with Angela when she was kidnapped?" Chris asked.

"Close enough to see what happened, but too far away to stop it. I would've gladly blown my cover to protect her, but there was nothing I could do from where I was."

"What was your cover?"

He paused. "I don't usually discuss that, but I think you deserve to know. Angela was pretending to be a job counselor for the refugees and I was acting like a company rep who hired people. That way we could talk periodically without causing suspicions. Onlookers would most likely think she was talking to me about job opportunities."

"We got a hit on Angela's RFID here." Chris nodded toward the door Nathan had exited. "What'd you find in there?"

Nathan looked surprised. "You what? How did you know about that? Has little Miss Perfect been telling secrets at home?"

"No. She never mentioned it." He didn't want to admit to hacking into MI6 computers. If they knew, they'd shut him out, or stop posting information about Angela's kidnapping. "What did you find?"

Nathan looked at him for seconds, as if trying to decide what to say. "We got a clue to come here. I searched the place and found nothing."

Chris knew Nathan was lying. The chip had been here. He probably didn't want to share information with the amateurs. "You said 'we.' How many of you are here?"

"I'm the only one here, on the ground, so to speak. The rest are supporting me from afar."

"How far afar?" Tex asked.

"London."

"And?" Chris asked. "Any drones overhead here?"

"Could be." Nathan's eyes narrowed.

Heinz hadn't said much so far. "That sounds like a 'yes' to me. Can you share with us what you found?"

Nathan looked at Heinz then turned to Chris. "Who's he?"

"Our interpreter." Chris said. "So, can you tell us what you've discovered?"

"Sorry. That's not up to me. In fact, if I don't check in soon, there's no telling what might happen. Home Office is a little jittery since Angela's abduction and they're watching the rest of us carefully. May I have my phones, please?"

Tex looked to Chris for his okay.

"I don't see why not." Chris turned to Nathan. "But stay out of our way. If you can't help us, we won't help you."

Chris pulled the RFID reader out of his pocket and turned it on. "Let's go, guys. We need to search this building."

The reader immediately flashed red and beeped. Louder than before.

Nathan started to walk away, but Chris grabbed him by the back collar of his coat. "He's got the chip."

CHAPTER ELEVEN

Chris moved the reader with its flashing red light closer to Nathan until he found the most likely place for Angela's RFID. He pointed. "Show me what's in that pocket."

Nathan didn't answer and didn't move. He looked toward the sky.

Chris pointed his gun at Nathan. "Now!"

Nathan looked into Chris's eyes, moved back, and held both hands out. "Look. This is not what you think."

"Really? Then, show me what you're hiding."

Chris looked toward Tex and nodded. Tex pulled his pistol out and aimed it at Nathan.

"Okay," Nathan said. "I've got the RFID chip. I didn't want to hurt you by showing it to you. You know what I mean. I didn't want you to think the worst, mate."

"Show me!"

Nathan pulled out the bra. The reader went crazy and so did Chris.

He jerked the bra from Nathan's hands and stuffed it in his pocket.

"Hey, I've got to take that back to the home office."

Chris hit Nathan's face with all the force he could muster. "Take *that* back to the home office."

Heinz moved in closer and caught Nathan who was off balance and reeling toward the ground. Chris wasn't sure if Heinz was there to help or stop him from hitting the British spy again.

Either way, there'd be no more punching. Angela wouldn't want her partner hurt, no matter what he'd done. Maybe he *had* hidden the chip to protect Chris. After all, it was in an intimate garment.

Liz held Chris's arm, and looked toward Nathan. "You lied to us. Please go."

Nathan rubbed his face. "I had no choice. We can't share criminal investigation information with . . . with people like you."

Chris grabbed the agent's arm. "The lady said to leave."

When Nathan stood still, his mouth open as if wanting to continue to talk, Chris grabbed the man's collar and compelled him to start moving.

When Nathan was a half block away, Liz went to Chris and wrapped her arms around him. "I think you need a hug, darling."

***

Chris's first thought was, they might as well go home. Not back to the minibus or the hotel, but to Bath and Texas. They'd failed. The RFID chip in his pocket was the only clue that could have led them to Angela.

But, as Liz applied her usual bear hug, it was as if she squeezed the negative thoughts out of his mind. By the time she let up, he knew he would find an answer. He *would* find Angela.

He gently moved away from Liz. "Thank you. I needed that."

Tex moved in close. "You look like you got a revelation. What do we do now?"

Chris laughed. Liz and Tex laughed along with him. Heinz's eyes opened wide. "What is funny?"

"Tex's question," Chris said. "He asked what do we do now and I have no idea. But we'll figure it out. We began without a plan and got this close to finding her. We can do it again. All we have to do is find where the kidnappers moved her."

"But, how?" Heinz asked.

Chris pondered the question. "The first thing that comes to mind is to see what Nathan does. Tex said according to the man's phone, he's not too fastidious about hiding information. Right, Tex?"

Tex removed his Stetson and grinned. "That's right. It'll be easier to watch him and perhaps get new clues. In addition, He'll probably file a report with MI6 as soon as he gets back to his hotel room."

Chris turned to Tex. "Did you hear what Nathan said about how he normally leaves his ID and phone in the safe? Remember the first time we met Angela?"

Tex nodded as he chuckled. "I do. She had no ID on her. Not even a driver's license . . . and she was driving a car in Texas. I remember thinking how gutsy that was. I grab my license to drive to the neighborhood grocery store."

"Right," Chris said. "So, here's another thing we can do. We'll find her hotel room and see if she left any clues behind."

Liz frowned. "How are we gonna do that? We don't know where she stayed, and, if we do find the hotel, we wouldn't know her room number. Besides, Nathan said he left his ID in the hotel room safe. We certainly don't know the combination to her safe."

"No problem," Chris said. "That'll slow us down some, but we can do it."

"Even safe combination?" Heinz asked.

Chris nodded. "Unfortunately, yes. There are several YouTube videos on how to open those particular safes."

Tex smiled. "Sounds like a plan. What's first?"

"First," Chris said, "let's head back to the minibus and use that fancy new computer to see if Nathan's filed his report yet."

Heinz looked at his wrist watch. "Uh . . . I need to make a call. You know, keep wife happy. I will meet you at the bus."

***

When everyone was back in the minibus, they stood in the control center while Chris assigned tasks. "Liz, would you open the library? It'll give us a reason to be parked here. There's no telling what Nathan might do. I'm not sure if he is aware of the type of vehicle we have, but if he is, I wouldn't be surprised if he called the police and reported us to get us out of his hair."

"What?" Heinz looked confused. "What is 'get out of his hair'?"

Liz laughed. "It's merely a saying. Like our being here is a nuisance for him." She moved toward the inner wall that separated the control center from the library. "I'll open the bookmobile. Has anyone seen a feather duster around here?"

Tex responded. "Nope. Maybe we can buy one somewhere. I know how much dusting books makes you happy."

Chris turned to Heinz. "Since you're the only one who understands the language, I'd like you to walk around the neighborhood watching and listening for anything out of the ordinary. Also, you might learn something that will give us a little warning if MI6 starts looking for us."

"I will. Could I watch you break a computer before I go?"

Chris paused. "You mean break *in* a computer?"

"Yes. That."

Tex turned toward the desk in the operations center. "Nothing to see but a bunch of numbers."

"Right," Chris said. "Go ahead and look around the

area and I'll show you how we break into computers when you get back."

"I go." Heinz pouted as he headed for the door.

"Keep that earpiece on in case we need to reach you," Chris added.

When Tex and Chris were alone in the control center, Chris took the computer on the right and nodded toward the one on the left. "You take that one."

"You okay?" Tex asked. "You don't sound like yourself."

"No. I'm not. But what can I do? We've got to keep searching. I'm never giving up. Not ever." He didn't mention his suspicions about Heinz. It was difficult to talk privately when the comm system was always on. Maybe he and Tex could get together later.

Chris had many questions. Why had the translator hung back to make a phone call? Why was he so interested in breaking into the MI6 computer? Could everything about the man that looked strange be explained?

Tex rolled in close to his assigned computer. "You know, finding a piece of her clothing doesn't mean anything bad happened to her."

"I know." Chris tapped Tex on the shoulder to get him to look at him then pointed to his ear piece.

Tex silently communicated. "Sorry."

Tex was the only person Chris could talk to about his feelings. If everyone hadn't been listening, he may have told Tex how overwhelmed he'd felt when Angela's clothing turned up. It was partly because he'd had his hopes up because of the RFID reader indicating the chip was near. Then, when Nathan hid the bra from him, Chris almost lost it.

He couldn't talk about his feelings, but he could discuss what happened. "I wonder if the kidnappers found the chip the same way we did. With a reader."

"Probably."

"That means they left it there to throw us off."

"Makes sense," Tex said.

"Can you hear me, Liz?"

"Sure can."

"Any customers?"

"Patrons, you mean. No. I'm the only one here."

"Okay. Let me know if anyone stops by."

"Will do."

"Heinz? You there?"

"Yes. I am walking around and looking for anything unusual. Haven't seen anyone yet."

"Okay, let us know if you see anything."

"I understand."

"Okay, Tex, it's time for us to get to work." Chris sat and adjusted the keyboard.

Tex moved his monitor in closer. "What do you want me to work on?"

Chris typed rapidly. "I'll check in with MI6 and see if they've posted any updates on Angela. See if you can log into our hotel Wi-Fi."

Tex's eyebrows rose. "Hotel Wi-Fi? What are we looking for?"

"First, see if you can find out where Nathan is staying."

"That should be easy. Like I said before, he doesn't

seem to worry much about security."

For the next few minutes all Chris could hear was the clickity clack of the keys from the two keyboards.

Tex stopped typing and Chris did too. "Find something?" he asked.

Tex shook his head. "Nothing I can tie to Nathan. Do you think we need to give him more time to access his computer?"

"Maybe," Chris said. "Or maybe he's in another hotel. We assumed he was staying the same place we are since it's the hotel closest to where Angela was abducted. They may have been in a different hotel."

"You want me to search other hotels nearby?"

"Yes. Perhaps Angela and Nathan both wanted some distance from the area they were investigating. Get Michael to help if you need him."

"Nah. I can do it." Tex's fingers flew across the keyboard. "Okay. First, I'll use the browser to show me all the hotels near ours. I can usually ID the Wi-Fi name by the hotel name. Some of these are in German. We should've kept Heinz here to help with the translation."

"I am here," Heinz said.

Tex laughed. "Oh, yeah. I forget you can hear everything we say."

"Me, too," Liz said.

"Yes, I can tell you what the Wi-Fi names mean," Heinz said.

Chris held up a hand only Tex could see. "Before doing that, would it help to physically move nearer to a hotel?"

Tex nodded. "Good idea. The hotels are clumped together." He pointed to the online map. "We could get a stronger signal if we moved in closer to where they are."

"Okay, Heinz and Liz. We need to move to the hotel."

"Okay," Liz said. "I'll prepare the bookmobile for travel."

"What do you want me to do?" Heinz asked.

"We'll wait for you to get back here," Chris said.

"Okay."

Tex turned off the speaker on his communications loop and indicated Chris should do the same. After he did, Tex spoke softly. "What's going on with Heinz?"

"What do you mean?"

"There's something in your voice. It's as if you don't trust him."

Chris thought about that. "I guess I don't."

"Why? What's he done?"

"Nothing specific. He's just so nosey for an interpreter."

"Is that all? I thought he was more than an interpreter. Didn't he say he was an investigator also?"

Chris nodded. "I guess, but something's not right."

The wall between the library and the control center opened and Liz walked in. "So, where we going?"

Chris flipped his comm switch back on and so did Tex. If Liz noticed, she didn't say anything.

"As soon as Heinz gets back, we'll move closer to the hotel so Tex can find Nathan and we can see what he's doing." Chris knew Heinz could hear this discussion, but it didn't matter. "I'd like to know what Nathan tells MI6."

Tex laughed. "He seems the type who'd use a hotel Wi-Fi for his secret work."

***

It wasn't long before Heinz returned and they moved the minibus closer to the cluster of hotels Tex had found with his browser.

Liz posted one of the signs their benefactor had left in the vehicle. *Abgeschlossen*, it said. Simple and to the point. Closed.

Everyone watched as Tex went through the hotel's Wi-Fi's, one network at a time, looking for guests who were logged on. Guests whose entries sounded like Nathan.

"Oops," Tex said.

"Did you find him?" Chris asked.

"Huh? Oh, no. Some idiot entered a credit card number and everything I need to use it. See that? Number, expiration date, special code, name and address of card holder, even his zip code. If people only knew how easy it was to see their data, they'd never use a hotel Wi-Fi again."

Liz's eyes widened. "I didn't know about that. Of course I don't use computers much anyway. Good thing, huh?"

Tex kept typing. He stopped suddenly and leaned in close to the screen. "Well, well. Looky here. I think

I've found him. I knew he wasn't too bright . . . about technology anyway."

"He was smart enough to get his office to block me." Chris looked at Heinz.

Heinz gave a brief glance toward Chris then turned to watch Tex.

Tex shook his head. "He must've had help with that. Here, he's using social media to post his status. No one is that dumb."

Chris moved in to read over his shoulder. "What'd he say?"

Tex grinned. "You know what? I bet the info I found in his phone is all fake. Look, he's logged in as Nathan Marlowe, same as I saw on his phone."

"What's he saying," Chris asked again.

"Get this," Tex said. "'Our winged friend has flown the coop.' He's talking about Angela. Angel? Wings?"

Chris stared at Tex's screen. "I agree. Get that hotel name and room number."

Tex scribbled the information on one of the three by five cards he carried in his left breast pocket. "Here it is."

"What are we going to do now?" Liz asked. "You're not going after Nathan, are you?"

Chris shook his head. "No. In fact, we should try to keep from being seen by him. Based on what Tex has found, there's a good chance his name is fictitious. The reason we tracked him down is to find Angela's room. They may have stayed at the same hotel."

"Oh," Liz said, "let me find her. Remember how I talked the desk clerk in London into letting me have a key to Cloris's room, may she rest in peace?"

"Yes," Chris said. "You did a good job there. It's different here. First, we don't know what name Angela used to register at the hotel."

Heinz cleared his throat. "Also, I think we should approach the desk clerk in his or her native language, which I am assuming is German. However, I speak five other languages if needed. You have a photo of your dear wife with you, I presume. With that and two-hundred euros I'll get her room number."

"I've got a photo," Chris said. "What's the money for?"

Heinz smiled. "Cooperation."

Chris thought for a minute. "Okay. Let's do it. Don't let Nathan see you, though. All I want you to do is find Angela's room number and come straight back. We'll take it from there. I don't want to be responsible for you getting accused of breaking and entering."

Tex pushed his hat back. "Yeah. That's *our* specialty."

"It's my wife's room," Chris said. "That would give me certain rights to enter. But, I may not be able to prove we're related."

Chris pulled out a wad of bills, counted out two hundred euros, and handed the money to Heinz. "Do you want to take more in case the clerk haggles?"

Heinz took the money and held it out. "Oh, he will haggle for sure, but this will be sufficient. If not, I will pay the rest and you can refund me. I have done this before, right here in Berlin. This seems to be the going rate. I will offer less, of course, then increase it as needed. And, I will return to you any money I do not use."

Chris walked Heinz to the door of the minibus to see him off, wondering again if he could be trusted. "We'll wait for you here. Good luck."

CHAPTER TWELVE

Two hours later Chris and Tex stood at the entrance to Angela's hotel room. Heinz had learned the room's location while staying within budget. The desk clerk provided more than a room number. He told Heinz the woman registered with a British passport as Charlene Frank. Chris didn't know if that information would be useful, but he stored it in his memory in case.

Tex had gotten Nathan's room number while searching the hotel's Wi-Fi data. Angela's room was on a different floor than Nathan's. Even so, Chris and Tex were careful on their way to her room, hoping not to run into Nathan and have to explain why they were there.

Because of the wheelchair, they had no choice but to use the elevator, and that increased their visibility.

Tex opened the door to Angela's room in a few seconds with the help of tools he carried in a manicure kit that was always in his wheelchair backpack.

Chris went in first, and took a deep breath. Her scent was there, albeit faint. It was strongest near a nightgown she'd left on a chair near the bed. He swallowed hard. "We better get busy. Nathan could show up here anytime. After our run-in with him, MI6 may decide to investigate her room, or check her out of the hotel."

Tex rolled to the dresser. "I'll search through everything here if you want to open that room safe."

Chris considered Tex's offer. "No need to take time to search now. Put everything in her suitcase and we'll look at it later when we're safely back to our hotel."

"Good idea. I'm for getting out of here as soon we can. Now that I'm married with two kids, I tend to be more careful when breaking the law."

Chris laughed. "Yeah. Especially in a foreign country."

Tex moved the suitcase to the bed and opened it. "You need any help with that room safe?"

"Maybe. But let me try first. Check around the room to see if there's anything else to pack. There may be makeup in the bathroom. We'll take everything Angela left."

Chris found the safe. "It looks promising. It's the same model we have in the States."

"Great."

Chris's memory allowed him to recall how to open this particular safe. He'd also read about how the security had been improved since the first YouTube video demonstrating how easy it was to break into hotel safes. He hoped this was one of the older models.

He knelt and followed the instructions as if he were reading the operating manual. He finished the last step in less than a minute.

Tex rolled over in time to see the safe door open. "Cool. You've got to show me how to do that."

"Why?"

"Oh . . . you know . . . for situations like this. Anything in there?"

Chris pulled out a handful of items and looked them over. "Yes. Her purse with ID, cash, and credit cards, and the usual stuff women carry around. This must be her phony purse, though. The photos are correct, but the name shown is 'Charlene Frank'."

"Anything else in there?"

"A phone. Did you see a charger in the room?"

"Yep. I packed it already."

"Makeup?"

"All packed."

Chris stood. "Okay, let's get out of here. We got what we came for. We can check it over when we get back to the minibus."

Tex added Angela's purse and the rest of the items found in the safe to the suitcase. Chris closed it and carried it to the door. He opened the door and held it for Tex. The elevator bell dinged.

"Uh-oh," Chris said in a whisper. "That could be Nathan checking on Angela's room. Let's go the other way.

Tex hesitated. "I need the elevator."

"I know," Chris said. "We'll come back here after he leaves. If it's him."

"Did you shut the safe?" Tex asked.

"No. I didn't think it would matter."

"Probably not. Unless Nathan goes in to look around. He'd probably know what should be in there."

"Too late to worry about that," Chris said. "It wouldn't be the end of the world if he saw us, but he might have some legal right to Angela's belongings since she was here on official government business. I don't want to find out."

They kept walking in the direction away from the elevators, still not knowing if Nathan was the reason the elevator stopped. They turned in when they got to an ice and vending machine area, and waited.

After a few minutes, Tex rolled into the hall and looked toward Angela's room. "I don't see anyone. How we gonna know when he's gone?" He rolled back over to where Chris was studying the vending machine choices.

"We won't. We'll wait, give him plenty of time."

A few minutes later Nathan walked in carrying an empty ice bucket.

If he was surprised to see them, he wasn't for long. "Gentlemen. I didn't know you were staying here. Nice place, huh?"

"Yes," Tex said. "Very nice."

Chris stared at Nathan's blackeye for too long before turning toward the vending machine. "Oh, hi. Do you know what coins we need for this machine?"

***

Nizar tossed a pile of black clothing to the backseat next to Angela. "You wear."

He looked as if he were prepared for a fight this time since Angela had refused to wear anything to cover her face before. He held a nine-inch rusty knife to Emma's neck and grinned. "You no wear. Me kill." He rubbed the blade on the young woman's face. "Too bad. Such pretty neck."

Angela decided the fight wasn't worth taking a chance on what Nizar might do. She pulled the burqa on over her clothes. He probably only needed her to wear it for the walk from the car to the building. After that she could take it off.

The other terrorists were out of the vehicle. Interestingly, Nizar seemed to hide his knife from someone. Was it Volker, the driver? The one who was wearing her GPS watch. Why would Nizar care what the driver thought?

Emma struggled to get her burqa on until Angela helped. They climbed out. Liliane took Emma's arm. Nizar took one of Angela's arms and Sayid the other.

Angela noticed Volker didn't walk with them toward the camp. Instead, he shook hands with Nizar and climbed back into the van. It was as if he were leaving, not merely moving the vehicle to a parking area. She wondered if the GPS watch would remain close to her or not.

Angela scanned the area as they walked. She

recognized the entrance to the Mitte Camp from photos she'd seen. The building they walked toward was separate from the main camp, more like a place for staff who worked at the camp, perhaps the home of a supervisor or a maintenance person. However, she noted there was a lock on the outside of the door. That made her think the place could be a supply room.

The distance from the van to the building with the lock on the door was about twenty feet. Angela didn't want to go into the locked building. She looked around for someone who might help her escape.

There had been few, if any, pedestrians at the Tempelhof Airport camp, but from what she'd read there should be private businesses and people outside this camp. Plus, the refugees were free to come and go without restriction.

If she screamed loud enough, would someone come to her aid? If they wouldn't help, they might at least call the police.

She didn't scream. And then it was too late. They made it to the building without seeing a single person.

Nizar looked at Angela and nodded toward the locked door. "Nice, yes?"

He unlocked a heavy-duty weathered Yale lock. The door handle itself didn't require a key. With a facetious bow, he held the door open for Angela and Emma to enter. "New home. Please."

Angela took one last look around. A car passed by on the street where the van had dropped them off. On the other side of the street was a laundromat. She saw no one to act as rescuer.

She walked through the opening and looked around the room. It *was* nice. For a prison. Angela thought of a cheap motel she'd stayed in while working on a case in Soho. The only difference was this place didn't have a window. Perhaps she'd been right about it being a supply room.

There were two single beds with military style folded blankets on each of the worn blue-striped mattresses. She had to admit this place was better than the dump where she and Emma had been held up until now. No longer would they be forced to smell the rotten food and stale beer that soaked the floors at the Tempelhof Airport camp.

Angela removed the burqa and tossed it on the floor. Emma did the same.

Nizar nodded toward one of the beds. "Good, huh." He looked at Angela and pointed his head again toward the bed, adding a vulgar gyration to his hips followed by a laugh that filled the room.

Angela pointed to the door they'd just entered. "Get out and leave us alone."

He harrumphed, but didn't leave. Instead, he walked to the other door in the room. "Toilet and sink. No drink water." He pantomimed the action as if his English wasn't good enough to be understood. "No drink. No brush." He made motions as if brushing his teeth.

"Does that mean we get toothbrushes?" Emma was suddenly interested in what was going on.

Nizar shrugged. He didn't understand or didn't care.

After he left, Angela listened for the padlock outside to click into place. She heard the sound, but, after giving Nizar time to leave, she tried to open the door anyway. It didn't bulge, not a crack to peek from.

Angela picked up the burqas and tossed one to Emma. "We probably should keep these. They may come in useful for bedcovers or pillows. Those mattresses don't look so clean."

Emma leaned in close to one of the beds. "Smells better than the floor we've been sleeping on."

Angela picked up a blanket and looked it over. "Emma, shake out your blanket before you use it. This one is dusty. Hope there are no bed bugs here."

"Yuk! Where do I shake it?" Emma didn't move.

Angela held out an arm. "Over there in that corner. As far away as possible."

Emma still didn't move. "I think I'd rather sleep on the floor."

Angela walked toward the bathroom. "Suit yourself. The mattress might be softer."

She checked the bathroom where they were told not to drink the water. There was a porcelain toilet covered with a brown stain up to the waterline. She pulled the handle to flush. The water went down slowly and the tank refilled. She looked for toilet paper, but didn't see any.

The sink next to the toilet produced only cold water. No tub, no shower. Angela wondered if they'd be allowed to use a communal shower or if this was all they'd have for cleaning up. A communal shower would offer opportunities to escape.

She touched every part of the two rooms, with her hands or her eyes, looking for a way out. The floor was dirty, worn carpet. She pulled up some at the corner to find vinyl tile over concrete beneath the carpet.

The walls were covered with plywood made to look like varnished wood. They could be removed by hand if she found a good reason to do so. Maybe the plywood covered windows. She'd check that later.

Emma was on her bed now, still holding the blanket she was supposed to shake out.

Angela shook out her own blanket in the corner then rested on the bed a few minutes. The ceiling was solid. No hanging ceiling tiles. Probably no attic. One lightbulb on the end of a hanging wire dangled from the middle from the ceiling. That could be useful.

She checked the bathroom and found a light in the center of the ceiling there, too. Just the wire itself would make a good weapon. An electrified one would be even better.

Next she listened, placed an ear to the back wall.

Emma sat up. "What are you doing?"

"I'm listening to see if anyone is in the area behind this room."

"Why?"

"Looking for a way to escape."

"Who are you, Charlene?"

"I told you. I'm a job counselor."

"But, you act like a . . . I don't know . . . a spy or something."

"Look. You don't have to be a spy to search for ways to get out of here. Just a survivor. I've studied self-defense, that's all."

"I don't think they would hurt us. Not seriously."

Angela moved away from the wall and stared into the young woman's eyes. "What makes you say that?" Surely Emma understood how dangerous their captors were.

Emma sat up. "I don't know. I guess I feel sorry for the refugees. That's why I was here. I wanted to help them. They've lost everything. Their families, their homes, their household goods, even their country."

Angela shook her head, wondering what Emma could be thinking. "I feel sorry for most of the refugees, too. But not the people holding us prisoners. They're not refugees. They're here to take advantage of the refugees."

Emma looked up. "I don't believe you. They can't help what they're doing. They're just trying to survive."

Angela sat next to Emma and put her arm around her like she would a little sister. "Let me tell you something. You're right. There are some victims in this camp and in all the refugee camps around here. But the people who abducted you and I are ISIS operatives sent here to recruit fighters, especially suicide bombers, a position that is getting harder and harder to fill."

Emma's eyes open wide. "What makes you say that?"

Angela paused, wondering if Emma could be a plant. No way. She was too naïve. Still, it was best not to tell her more than she needed to know. Only enough to make her cautious. "Before I left England to take my job here as a job counselor I was given instructions to watch out for ISIS recruiters." Part of that was true.

"Based on what's happened to us, I believe these people fit the description I was given. Why else would they keep us confined?"

Emma swallowed hard. "For ransom?"

"Yes. But, a refugee wouldn't have a way to do that. A refugee wouldn't have a car, a team of helpers, and the ability to find a place to hide us. Nor would a refugee have the means to contact your parents or my company and set up an exchange of us for money."

Emma was silent.

"Do you understand what I'm saying?" Angela turned to face the young woman.

The nod began slowly than increased as if the idea was finally getting to Emma. "You're frightening me. What . . . what do we do?"

Finally. "I don't know yet, but I believe someone will be looking for us soon. If they're not already."

"Your company?"

"Yes." That was mostly true, too. "And, when they do—"

The padlock on the door to the outside jiggled, announcing a visitor.

Angela whispered, "If that's one of the guards, be strong. They don't know how to react to strong women. Understand?"

Emma nodded her head just as the door opened.

Liliane stood in the doorway, carrying a canvas bag. "Food. Water." She placed the bag on one of the beds and reached in and pulled out a roll of toilet paper with only about a quarter of the tissues remaining. She smiled as she held it out. "Good?"

"Thank you." Angela took the roll. She wanted to say more, perhaps get Liliane to help them, but she wasn't sure if they could trust her.

Liliane used her hand and fingers to say what Angela determined meant do not flush the paper. "Okay, we won't flush the paper."

Emma looked alarmed. "What? Why?"

"Probably a septic tank that's near full. It'll be okay." Angela had been sent to many places that didn't allow toilet paper to be flushed.

Liliane smiled. She probably understood more English than she could speak. She turned and left. The sound of the lock snapping into place was clear.

CHAPTER THIRTEEN

Chris lifted Angela's suitcase onto the minibus and then helped Tex with the lift. Liz and Heinz met them in the operations control section.

Liz nodded at the suitcase. "Well, I see you got into her room. Any problems?"

Chris chortled. "Everything went fine until we got ready to leave. That's when we heard the elevator bell and went to hide in the vending machine room in case it was Nathan. But, unfortunately, that's where he was heading. Lucky for us, he didn't seem surprised we were there. He assumed we were staying in the hotel. He should have wondered why we had a suitcase with us in the vending machine area, but he didn't ask. Not too smart for a spy."

Liz was puzzled. "Nathan probably recognized his

partner's baggage. I bet they traveled together before."

Tex wiped a large white handkerchief around the inside of his Stetson. "I parked my chair between him and the suitcase so maybe he didn't see it. If he did, he didn't act like he recognized it. Some men don't notice things like that. You know, clothes, hair, and stuff. Luggage qualifies as stuff men don't see."

"That is true," Heinz said, "but this person is trained to observe everything around him. Is he not?"

Chris pushed his keyboard back and placed Angela's suitcase on the desk. "That's correct, he probably figured out what happened by now. But there's not much we can do about it. Deed's done. We got caught. Sort of. It either won't matter or they'll come after us. None of that will change what we do next." Chris unzipped the suitcase and lifted the lid up until it propped against his monitor.

Tex looked at the open bag. "What *do* we do next?"

"All we can do is search for clues."

Liz reached into the suitcase and took out Angela's clothes. "Chris, you might want to check this stack for those RFID chips."

"Yes. Thank you, Liz." Chris went through the clothing and set it aside when he was done.

Tex looked in the emptied grip. "Not much left. Only her purse, phone, and phone charger. Oh, and some papers."

"Was all that in the room?" Liz asked.

Tex nodded. "Chris found the phone and Angela's purse in the room safe. The charger was plugged in a wall outlet."

Liz helped Tex remove the purse, phone and charger and place them on the desk. "What did you say about some papers?"

Heinz peeked at the papers in the suitcase. "Probably not too important or she would have put them in the safe."

Chris took the papers and examined them. "This is mostly computer printouts of websites describing refugee camps in Germany. Probably no need to hide them since she was ostensibly there to help refugees find work. Let's save it, though. Perhaps *we* can use this information."

Liz picked up a thin book that fell from the letter-sized pages of printout. "What's this?"

Tex took the booklet from Liz. "This is a user manual for Garmin Forerunners, 'a GPS-enabled running watch' it says." He held the manual where Chris could see the cover photo showing the watch. "Did she wear this at home?"

Chris studied the cover, looked inside, and handed it back to Tex. "No. I haven't seen anything like that before. She didn't wear a watch. I didn't know she owned one. Could be something she wears at work, or something she got for this assignment." He turned to Tex. "If she's wearing this watch, can we find her location?"

"Let me see." Tex scanned the booklet. "Yes! It says friends and family can keep up with a person who is wearing the watch."

"That's what we need," Liz said. "Does it explain how?"

Heinz nodded. "This could be why the Nathan guy did not seem too concerned about Angela when he found the chip. They had a backup method of tracking her. I bet they know where she is now."

Chris couldn't help feeling relieved at the thought of MI6 knowing where his wife was, but he was angry Nathan hadn't shared the information. "Is that right, Tex? Can *we* find her?"

Tex stared at the manual. "Hmm. Only if she gives permission."

Chris took the user's manual from Tex and read the page Tex had been reading. "The user must log on to the website indicated and enter the email address for all those she wants to allow access to her location. All we have to do is add our email address."

"I know," Liz said. "You're gonna hack the watch company's website."

Chris smiled, flipping the manual over. "Well, I suspect I could do that. But, to save time, and knowing my wife, I think we should first try logging in with her ID and password, both of which are written on the back cover of this manual."

Tex grabbed the manual, laughed, and started typing. It wasn't long before he laughed louder. "Yes. That was a lot easier." He pointed to the screen. "Here we can see where the watch is right at this moment."

Everyone moved closer. "Where is she?" Chris asked.

Tex looked up toward Chris, no longer laughing. "Doc, we don't know it's her. All we know is it's her watch."

"I know. Where is *it*?"

"The watch is moving toward us at a rapid speed, at least eighty miles per hour."

"How far away?" Heinz asked.

Chris looked back to the screen, pointed to a map. "See the blue dot? That's the location of the watch. It's on the A9 near Leipzig, going north toward Berlin."

"Is moving fast," Heinz said, "but, still about two hours from here."

"It may not be coming here," Tex said. "The driver could turn off anywhere along the way."

Chris looked up, stretched, and then addressed the others in his best college professor voice. "Tex is right. We don't know if this is Angela or only her watch. Either way, I want to know I've done everything I can to find her. So, here's what I suggest."

He pointed at the map on the screen. "We're here and the watch is there. Heinz says we're two hours apart. What if we head south on the A9 and meet in the middle? That'll cut the time to one hour and we'll be in a better position in case they turn off somewhere along the way. Okay? I'll drive. We'll open the door between the library and the control center so we can communicate directly."

"What'll we do when we get to where the watch is?" Liz asked.

Chris turned to Tex. "Is that GPS system good enough to let us know which vehicle the watch is in?"

"Sure."

"Good." Chris ran his fingers through his beard. "There's one problem. Autobahns such as the A9 don't have access roads the way we have in the States. That means when we get to the vehicle carrying the watch we may have to continue driving for miles before we can turn around and follow it."

"That is true." Heinz held a hand out toward the screen. "But there is a way. Service areas let you change directions. See, here's one." He pointed again. "There another. We can watch the vehicle and be in one of the service stops ready to go north when the vehicle reaches us. A bit longer it will take, but at least we will not lose the vehicle with the watch. That could happen if we go too far south before we can turn around."

"That'll work," Tex said.

Chris opened the door leading to the library section of the minibus. "Let's go. Tell me when to get off the A9."

***

Each morning in captivity, Angela worked to keep herself strong. Pushups. Running in place. Yoga. One day, in the middle of her exercise routine, she realized she was pregnant.

She'd suspected it the first day after she'd been kidnapped, but now she was convinced. Although being held captive could cause some of the same symptoms, she was bloated, fatigued, and nauseated, all indicators, she'd read, could be signs of pregnancy.

Being pregnant changed everything. It was like having another person to protect and to help escape. A person more important to her than anything in the world.

Emma vocalized each morning. She'd told Angela she had to warmup before rehearsing arias she'd memorized for an upcoming opera. Other times she sang some from operas she'd performed already. Some in other countries, and in several languages. On the same day Angela knew she was pregnant, Emma didn't sing and was still in bed when Liliane delivered food and water.

Liliane looked at Angela and nodded toward Emma. "Sick?"

Angela shrugged. She thought how best to talk to her keeper and gain her trust. "Mostly homesick. Any chance we can send her home? She misses her family and friends."

Emma looked up.

Liliane's eye opened wide. "Oh, no." She shook her head. "No, no, no."

She turned to Emma and placed a hand on the young woman's forehead. "I hear you sing. Beautiful singing. Must sing again today."

Emma turned toward her captor, and slowly moved her head from left to right.

Angela's mind went into high gear. She thought how easy it would be to overpower Liliane. The padlock was open. All she had to do was gag Liliane, tie her up and they could be gone in an instant. But, then what? Were there guards nearby? Did they have weapons? Were they watching the door?

While Liliane was busy with Emma, Angela opened the door and looked out. There were no guards outside, at least none she could see. The laundromat was across the street and she saw a woman go in carrying a bag of clothes. A car drove by on the street between the locked room and the laundry. Freedom was close. All she had to do was . . .

"No!" Liliane ran to the door where Angela stood looking out.

Angela took a deep breath and held up both hands. "I needed some fresh air. I'm not going anywhere." She took another breath as if to show her captor what she meant.

"You stay in room."

Angela walked away from the door. "Don't worry. I wasn't going to run. I won't do that. I won't get you in trouble." Angela watched for reaction from the woman.

Liliane stared back a few seconds longer before she turned toward Emma who was propped up on one elbow on her bed. "You sing now?"

Emma shook her head.

Liliane positioned herself on the edge of the bed where she could keep an eye on Angela while she talked with Emma. "You nice singer. Sweet voice."

"Thank you."

"Everyone outside listen when you sing. Miss it today."

Angela wondered if Liliane's concern for Emma would provide an opportunity for escape. She didn't want to leave Emma, but she was beginning to think it might be the only way to save her baby.

**

As they headed south on the A9, Chris watched for the next service area. He couldn't exit unless Tex gave him the go ahead. Tex had to determine which vehicle driving toward them carried Angela's GPS watch. And he had to do so soon enough to match up with a service stop that provided a way for them to reverse direction. It'd be a lot easier if Germany had service roads alongside the Autobahn the way Interstates did in much of the United States.

Chris nodded at Liz. "Liz, would you mind asking Tex if he has any idea how far it is until we turn around. I don't want to miss the exit."

"Ask him yourself on the comm."

"I pulled it out of my ear. It was beginning to bother me. Do you mind? Get him to show you so you can help me find the right exit."

"Oh, okay." Liz walked toward the rear of the bus.

When Liz was gone, Chris held an index finger against his lips. "Heinz, would you get my Glock and bring it to me?"

Heinz removed his comm and bent over to look out the window. "Why? Something is wrong?" He spoke in a whisper

"I'm not sure. I didn't want to alarm Liz, but we've had the same car on our tail for miles. It passed us once, then dropped back and stayed behind us."

"Probably not something to worry about. It could be the police checking our license plates. This bus is not exactly where it should be."

Chris threw a quick glance toward Heinz. "Where

are we supposed to be?"

"According to the license plates, we should be in Darmstadt. Except for some special plates, the licenses begin with a one to three letter abbreviation which represents the city or region where the vehicle is registered. B for Berlin, for example."

"Seems weird that would interest police. Can't people go anywhere they want?"

"Yes. True. But a library bus should stay in one city, mostly."

"Okay. Bring me my gun. I feel something is wrong and I want to be prepared."

Liz returned as Heinz opened the cabinet behind the driver's seat. "Gun? What are you talking about?"

"Nothing. What'd Tex say?"

"He said to take the next exit and we'll wait there for the suspect vehicle to show up. Now, listen. I don't like weapons. You know that. They're dangerous."

"Sorry, Liz. My intuition says I may need mine. Trust me on this."

Heinz handed the Glock to Chris. "Exit here."

Chris accepted the gun and placed it in a beverage holder. "Yeah. And when we do, I bet that car following us exits, too."

Chris turned off the Autobahn into the service area. The car that had stayed behind the minibus for so long drove on past the exit.

"Your intuition is proved wrong," Heinz said.

Liz laughed.

Chris shook his head. He didn't know Heinz that well and Heinz didn't know him, but those who did had learned to trust his intuition.

Chris looked around the service stop and could see a restaurant, hotel, and gas station. "Okay. What do we do now? We need to reverse direction."

Heinz looked out the front window. "Take the next left turn. That will lead us to the other side of the A9 where we can head north. Get near the access ramp, but not in it. Find a place to park. Tex will let us know when the vehicle with the GPS arrives."

When they were parked near the ramp to get back on the Autobahn to follow the suspects' vehicle, Heinz stepped out for a smoke. Chris noticed Heinz also made a phone call, prompting Chris to wonder once again if their interpreter could be trusted.

While they waited, Chris put his comm back on.

"He's getting close," Tex said. "Are you ready?"

"Heinz, we're leaving." Chris waited, but there was no response. Heinz hadn't turned his comm on.

Chris honked. Heinz stomped out his cigarette, jumped into the minibus and shut the door. Chris shifted into first gear, his feet on the clutch and brake pedals. "All set."

"Go." Tex's voice was strong, the way it got when things went according to plan.

Chris checked the traffic before accelerating onto the A9. "Did anyone see what kind of vehicle we're following?"

"Not yet," said Tex, "but we should be able to spot it soon. According to the computer display, I think it's in our lane, less than 100 yards ahead of us. What do you see there?"

Chris told Heinz, "If this is the right vehicle, it's a work-type van, with no windows in the back. It's old, rusty, dark brown or black." He paused. "I'm moving up closer."

"Tex said it is the one. He shows us on its tail."

Chris nodded. "Okay, I'm going to back off. I'll even change lanes from time to time so he won't get suspicious. Tell Tex not to lose him."

"Tex said move up on the side to where you can see how many people are in the vehicle."

"Okay." Chris pulled out to pass the van, slowing when he could see the driver. "There's no one in the passenger seat, but I can't see if anyone is behind the driver. I think we should pull him over and investigate."

Heinz didn't relay what Chris said. Instead, he gave Chris his opinion. "Someone stole the watch. That person could lead us to Angela. But not if we stop him too soon. Should we not follow him to his destination? If he will not talk, we will at least know something about where he went."

Liz nodded. "Makes sense."

Chris knew Heinz and Liz were right, but waiting was difficult and getting harder to do each day. He wanted answers now. He wanted Angela to be safe and in his arms. "Okay. Talk to Tex. Work out a plan when to apprehend this character. And make it soon."

CHAPTER FOURTEEN

The van they followed exited near the Tempelhof Airport camp. Chris suspected that would happen, but feared it wouldn't.

The van stopped and parked near a run-down hotel a few blocks from their nicer lodging.

Chris pulled the minibus over to the curb a good half-block distance from the van. "Heinz, since you speak the language, go delay the driver. That'll give us time to get Tex down in the lift and onto the pavement. Liz, stay here and watch the minibus."

Heinz nodded. "The driver looks German, but we can't be sure until we meet with him. What if he speaks only Arabic?"

"Find out. We'll be there shortly."

Heinz jumped out the front door of the minibus

and walked toward the van.

Liz patted Chris on the shoulder. "Leave your weapon here."

Chris placed his Glock under his shirt and inside the waistband of his pants. "No. But don't worry. I'll be careful."

Chris and Tex moved toward the spot where Heinz and the driver stood outside the van. Chris wasn't sure what was said, but they were both smiling. The stranger spoke German fluently, using his hands flamboyantly all the while.

When Tex and Chris got close to the two men, the driver moved back to allow room for Tex's wheelchair to pass. When Tex stopped instead, the man stared with raised eyebrows.

Heinz broke the tension. "Das sind meine Freunde."

"Ah, your friends. *Guten Tag*," the man said, holding out his right hand.

"This is Volker Dohr," Heinz said in English. "He is a delivery man. The van is his own. He will deliver anything for anyone as long as it is legal to do so."

"I bet." Anger swept over Chris. "Looks like he's wearing a stolen watch. Ask him about that."

The man understood English because he looked at his wrist and backed away from Chris.

"Is okay," Heinz said, nodding toward Chris, and speaking in English. "It is that his wife had a watch like yours and now she is missing."

The man replied in English, holding his arm out to show the watch. "This? I did not know it was stolen."

"Where did you get it?" Tex asked.

"I deliver merchandise. Usually small packages. Sometimes I am taxi. That is all. The people I work for sometimes give me things instead of money. That is where I got this watch." He took it off, making a big ritual out of returning the watch and handed it to Chris. "Here. It is yours."

Chris took it. "Who gave you the watch?"

Volker looked at Heinz as if waiting for his guidance.

Heinz put an arm on Volker's shoulder. "Is okay. We are not police. We do not care what you deliver or who you work for. We only want to find the person who gave you the watch. We will pay you for your time."

Volker looked at each one.

Heinz's voice had an urgency to it. "Do not worry. You can trust us. Tell us where you got the watch."

"Naturally I remember who gave me the watch. It was odd because the man always had money to pay. He had no reason to barter for my services. I was surprised, but I didn't want to hurt his feelings. Besides, I liked the watch so I took the gift from him."

"What were you paid to do?" Heinz asked.

"The night I got the watch I drove two men and three women from the Tempelhof Airport Camp to the Mitte Camp."

Chris moved closer to Volker. "Were the women taken by force?"

Volker looked surprised. "No. Of course not. I would never do such as that. They did not say anything, but they were not bound or gagged if that is what you mean. I think they slept most of the way."

"Who hired you to deliver the people to Mitte Camp?"

Volker didn't answer, looking left then right as if he might be watched.

Heinz patted the man's back. "Is okay to tell us. We will never betray you."

Volker looked into Heinz's face, pleading. "Please. He is my best customer. I need to work. To feed my family. Do not tell him I said this. I deliver sealed envelopes for him from one refugee camp to another, and, like I said, sometimes people as well."

"You can trust us," Heinz said. "What is the man's name?"

"Amin. I think it is Reyaad Amin."

"Where can we find this Amin?" Chris asked.

"I don't know. He calls me when he has something he wants delivered and then meets me at the clothes washing store near the camp. I think he lives at the refugee camp."

"Do you have a mobile number for him?" Heinz asked.

"No. He calls me and the caller ID is blocked."

"So, you meet at the laundry?" Chris asked.

"Yes. Since he moved to this camp. Before, we met other places. It is across the street from the main entrance to the camp." Volker looked at Chris as if waiting for another question.

Chris didn't disappoint him. "When you delivered the two men and three women, did you see where they were taken?"

"The Mitte Camp."

"Yes, but where in the camp?"

"I don't know that. I watched them go toward the front gate. Where they went after that is difficult to know."

"Will you deliver something for us?" Chris asked.

"Naturally."

Chris handed him the watch. "Take this and wear it. If you see the women again, give the watch to them without letting the men know."

"Okay. I assume you mean the Western women."

"What do you mean?"

"One was Middle Eastern. The other two were Western."

"Yes, the Western women. The one with the dark hair." Chris handed Volker some euros. "Will you deliver the watch?"

He looked at the roll of bills. "Yes. If possible. I may not see the woman again."

"Then, you may keep the watch."

"I promise to wear the watch and give it to the dark-haired Western woman if I ever see her again."

"Also, would you take this phone number and call us next time you are scheduled to meet Reyaad Amin?"

Volker looked at the bills again. "Certainly."

"Good. Now, may I see the back of the van?" Chris knew he wouldn't find anything there, but he had to look to be sure.

Volker opened the side door of the van and signaled for Chris to look.

***

"I'm *hongry*," Tex said in his best Texas accent when they got to the hotel. "Anyone want to join me for a bite to eat?"

"I'm in," Liz said. "I can't remember when we ate last."

"Me, too," Heinz said.

Chris was surprised they were hungry. He considered asking if they could skip a meal and help come up with ideas to find Angela. But, eventually, he reasoned that they could all think better with a good meal, including himself. That didn't mean they should waste more time than was necessary. Eat and go, that was enough. He wasn't hungry, but he went with them to the hotel restaurant.

Halfway through their meals, a phone rang. Chris didn't recognize the ringtone and no one moved to answer. The sound seemed to be coming from behind Tex. "Hey. Your backpack is ringing."

Tex shrugged, then reached around to the back of his wheelchair and retrieved a phone from the backpack. "Hmm. It's Angela's. I charged the battery while we were on the Autobahn and forgot all about it." He pressed a button. "Hello."

Tex pulled the phone from his ear, looked at it, then tried again. "Hello. Anyone there? I guess they didn't want to talk to me," he said.

Chris pointed at the phone. "Does it show a number?"

Tex looked. "No."

"It could be a wrong number," Heinz said.

Liz chimed in. "Maybe they were expecting a woman to answer. Next time it rings, give it to me."

Chris took the phone and looked at it. "This is her work phone. It was in the hotel room safe. Unless the kidnappers somehow learned the phone number, then the caller had to be MI6. Most likely Nathan." He pressed the call back button and held the phone to his ear. "It's not a working number. Funny. It was a minute ago. I bet it was Nathan."

Heinz cleared his voice the way he often did before speaking. "Or, someone selling something."

Chris looked at Heinz, wondering if he could be trusted. He'd made several private phone calls lately, and after one call, Chris was no longer able to retrieve information in the MI6 computer.

Coincidence, perhaps, but Chris didn't trust many people. He decided to keep an eye on Heinz. He'd talk to Tex later about his suspicions and see what he thought. Tex was often better at reading people than Chris was.

Chris passed the phone to Tex. "Have you had time to check this phone to see if there are any clues regarding where she might be?"

"When I had time, the battery was totally drained. Now that it's charged, I'll study it and let you know what I find. However, I can see there's an unsent text message addressed to you."

Chris's heart skipped a beat. "Really? What does it say?"

Tex looked at the phone's screen as if preparing to read a long message, then looked at Chris. "It says 'I love you.'"

Chris looked at him. "You're not just saying that, are you?"

"No, look." Tex held the phone where Chris could see the screen.

"Aw, that's nice." Liz looked like she had tears in her eyes.

"It was unsent?" Chris asked. "I wonder why?"

"I don't know," Tex said. "Perhaps she had it ready to go for when she got back to the hotel the day she was nabbed."

Chris usually worked only with facts and didn't consider negative possibilities without proof, but he couldn't help thinking she may have been interrupted before she hit send.

"Could be," Liz said. "Seems strange though. Had she texted you recently, during this assignment?"

"No. But that wasn't unusual. While she was away on business, we talked occasionally, but never very much. Sometimes she'd send a brief text. I've gotten the 'I love you' one many times. You'll find some from me to her when you check it over. This time things were different. I don't know why. She never tells me what she's doing. Part of the reason I panicked and called you all in to help was because I hadn't heard from her as usual."

Chris came to a decision during their meal, or perhaps after Angela's phone rang. It was time to move. While walking out of the restaurant, Chris announced, "Prepare to check out in the morning. We need to get closer to Mitte Camp where Volker took Angela."

"Good idea," Liz said. "Should we make reservations?"

"Yes," Chris said. "I'll get Michael to do that for us. I think we could all use a good night's sleep and Michael keeps asking for more to do."

When Chris got back to his room, he called Michael and explained the situation. "We can use some help, but it's not challenging."

"That's okay. Tell me." Michael sounded so eager, Chris wished he had something more exciting for him.

"We need hotel reservations near Mitte Camp."

"Okay. I know where the camp is. Four rooms?"

"Right."

"Anything else?"

"That's it." Michael was so efficient, Chris started to hang up. "You doing okay?"

"Yes. Taking care of the bookmobile service and the farm duties. Very exciting here. You?"

"We've had more dead-ends than successes, but we haven't given up."

"I understand. Let me know if I can help more."

Chris wished he had a good lead for Michael to work on. Of all the students he'd had over the years, Michael showed the most promise for becoming a top-notch white-hat hacker. "Will do."

"Good. I'll email your hotel information."

"Thanks. Goodnight."

***

Angela continued to look for ways to escape. They were alone in the room most of the time so there were plenty of opportunities to prowl. Inside, at least.

Angela watched for another chance to look outside each time Liliane was there. Each time Angela peeked out the door, Liliane fussed, but she allowed Angela more time at the door each time Liliane brought them food.

When Angela examined the fake wood wall covering, she found an electrical socket that was probably hidden during the last renovation. After making sure it wasn't hot, she pulled out about six feet of wire.

She thought of uses for her find. A way to tie Liliane's hands. A weapon of sorts, like a whip, or a garrote. Or, she could connect it to a live wire to shock someone. The possibilities were countless.

Angela hid the wire in her bedsprings, easily seen by someone looking, but not noticeable during Liliane's routine visits. Besides, if someone started to look there, Angela could move in, grab the six-foot length of electrician's wire from the springs and use it to garrote or restrain them.

Today's search involved the floor. Angela crawled around, searching for anything out of the ordinary under the carpet. What she found was that the floor was concrete covered with cheap, cracked vinyl which in turn was covered by dirty carpet. She didn't expect to find a way to escape through the floor, but, she kept looking. There might be an old, forgotten, opening somewhere under all the carpet and vinyl.

"Are you still trying to find a way to escape?" Emma sounded whinier than usual.

"Yes. Want to help me?"

"Not really."

"Okay. You're missing all the fun. It's good exercise, too. For your brain and your body."

It wasn't long before Emma was on the floor with Angela. "I'm sure this is a complete waste of time, but I'm so bored. Tell me what to do."

Angela patted the floor next to her. "Like this. Feel."

Staying busy was good for them. They might not find anything. But they'd never escape if they gave up and slept all day.

Emma plopped down and rubbed her hand over the floor in front of where she sat. "It feels like a filthy floor. Not even a vacuum cleaner could pry this grime off."

Angela lifted the carpet. "Check how solid it is under the vinyl?"

Emma pushed on the floor. "It's hard."

"Good. What we're looking for is a soft spot."

"Why?"

"This room has been remodeled, probably several times over the years. I've found electrical outlets under the wall panels. I think there could be openings under these floor coverings. Perhaps large enough to crawl through."

"Yuk. You mean like a sewer line?"

"Maybe. Or, we could find a basement or a workspace under the building. A place our captors don't know about."

Emma was up on her hands and knees moving around and checking the floor for signs of softness faster than Angela had done. Angela loved that Emma was doing something other than sleep. She'd worried about her young friend lately.

Three loud knocks sounded on the door. It couldn't be Liliane. She never knocked.

Angela tensed and walked to the door. "Who is it?"

From the other side of the door, she heard a loud voice say, "It is Reyaad Amin to see Charlene Frank. I'm coming in." The familiar sound of the padlock being unlocked announced his entrance.

Emma looked at Angela with twisted brows. "Is he a friend?"

CHAPTER FIFTEEN

The next morning, Chris was happy to see the email message from Michael had arrived.

On their way to the new hotel, Chris drove with Heinz in the passenger seat giving directions and translating signs when needed. Tex and Liz found seats in the bookmobile section as well. It was an opportunity for the four of them to talk.

Chris spoke first. "Tex, did you find anything useful on Angela's phone?"

"It was pretty clean. About what you'd expect for someone in her line of work." Tex pulled out the phone and turned it on. "It's the contact list that bothers me."

"Why?" Chris checked the side mirrors before changing lanes.

"There is only one person listed. And, he has no

phone number."

"What is the name?" Chris asked.

"Reyaad Amin., the name Volker mentioned."

"Any other information?" Chris asked.

"Title is Recruiter."

Heinz turned to face Tex. "Volker did not say *recruiter*."

"Maybe he didn't know," Tex said.

Liz flipped the page of the *USA Today* she'd been perusing. "The fact that Amin is in Angela's contact list and is the guy who hired Volker to drive Angela to Mitte Camp can't be a coincidence. It sounds like she was looking for him and he found her first."

"I wonder," Tex said, "is it possible Angela was working some type of deep cover operation and she partnered up with Reyaad Amin whether he knows who she is or not?"

Chris felt the hair on the back of his neck tingle. "You're saying maybe she wasn't abducted after all?"

"I don't know," Tex said. "Just thinking out loud."

"*Nein.*" Heinz said. "Not possible. Her partner saw the kidnapping. He found the RFID chip . . . "

"Yes," Tex said, "but if Angela was working with Amin, Nathan would know. And, if so, he lied about it."

Chris pulled to the curb near the new hotel Michael had found for them. What Tex proposed was conjecture, of course, but Chris didn't know what to think. At times like this his OCD kicked in. As a result, he straightened the minibus three times trying to get the vehicle parallel with the curb. "How does this look,

Liz? Are we close enough to the curb on your side?"

She didn't look out to check. "We're fine. The question is, are you okay? You're not having trouble with *you-know-what* are you?"

He turned off the engine and stared into her eyes trying to decide how to answer. She was one of a handful of people he'd talked to about his OCD problems. "I'll be okay. I was thinking about what Tex said."

He put the hand brake on and stood. "Tex, you gave us something to think about, but I believe faking an abduction would put her in harm's way for little advantage. I believe she was kidnapped and I want to continue as if that is the case."

Tex shrugged. "I saw a kidnapping faked on TV once and it seemed to work."

"This isn't TV," Chris said, ending the conversation.

He filed away Heinz's defense of Nathan and wondered once again if their interpreter was who he claimed to be.

They checked into the hotel and talked about meeting for dinner. Chris suggested they skip eating and go check on the refugee camp, but everyone seemed to want to wait until morning to start fresh.

When Chris finally got to his room for the night, he called Michael. "I'm sorry if I woke you. I sometimes forget you are so far away."

"That's okay. Call anytime. I want to help."

"Good. I appreciate that. I've got a job for you. Keep this off the comm. That means don't talk to me or anyone else about it unless we turn off our units."

"Sounds serious."

"Yes. It could be. Don't know. I want you to check out our translator. His name is Heinz Gabriel."

"Anything in particular you want to find out?"

"No. My intuition tells me he's not being honest with us."

"I suspect his name is not unique, especially in that part of the world. How will I know which Heinz Gabriel to investigate?"

"Hmm. I don't know. Look for translators in Berlin. I can send you a photo if that will help."

"It might. Where'd you get a photo?"

"I sneaked it one day while he thought I was talking on my phone. It's not a great photo."

"Might help. But, he may not be on the internet at all. I'll look around and let you know."

"Oh, I wonder if you might find something about him on MI6's network."

"Maybe. Don't forget they blocked us, though. I'll see if I can find another way in. While we're talking, there's another job I want to ask about."

"What's that?" Chris was satisfied with every job Michael had done for him.

"When I was looking around for a hotel, I saw the refugee camp. It's huge. If you like I can get a feel for the area and let you know the best places to look for Angela."

Chris took a deep breath, wondering why he hadn't thought of that. "Brilliant idea. Do it."

***

The next day, after Chris parked the minibus on the street near the front of the Mitte refugee camp, Tex sat at the computer desk in the control center with a view of the camp's main entrance on one monitor and the front of the laundromat across the street from the camp on the other.

The laundry's plate-glass window allowed them to see inside the building. There wasn't as much to see on the monitor showing the refugee camp.

Liz looked over his shoulder at one screen and then the other. "Neat! How'd you do that?"

Tex grinned. "Like it? It helped that we could park so close to the camp. When we were at the Tempelhof we had to park so far away we couldn't see the entrance from the street. We need to keep an eye on the laundry because that's where Volker goes when he meets with Amin."

Liz made a face. "I get all that. But how did you set up the computer to show what's going on in both places at the same time?"

Tex laughed. "How? Well, I had a little help from Chris. He climbed to the top of the bus and duct-taped the flex cameras in place, one pointing toward the camp and the other aimed at the laundry. Then all we had to do was send the video to the computer. We're not only watching in real time, we're recording it in case we want to look backward in time."

"I love it." Liz gave him a hug. "Where is Chris?"

Tex looked out the window. "After he taped the

flex cameras in place, he said he'd be back soon. I think he's walking around the area, getting a feel for the place."

"And Heinz?"

"Over there by the tree. Cigarette and phone. I think he checks in with his wife frequently. Of course I call Jane every day, too. But usually when we get back to the hotel."

"Sure wish we could get him to quit smoking. That stuff's deadly. I see more people smoking here than in the States."

"I noticed that, too. I had the habit for years, so I know it's hard to quit. We can talk to him and offer to help."

"Maybe I will. Course, I haven't stopped Samuel from smoking his pipe. Anything I can do to help you?"

"Nah. Not now. I think Chris might need you, though. He said something about getting you to do some laundry."

"Really? The female does the laundry, huh?" She laughed. "We'll see about that."

Tex hoped she wasn't upset. "Relax. He's going to ask you to check out the laundromat. They call it *Waschsalon* here. Chris wants you to find out what kind of coins are needed and if they sell detergent. We want to be prepared to go in when Volker calls and tells us he's meeting Amin. The laundromat camera will show us what's happening, but it won't pick up speech. That'll be your job. But, don't worry. When the time comes to go in to spy on Volker and Amin, maybe

Heinz should go with you for protection. I can go instead of you if you want me to."

Liz laughed. "Oh, I'm kidding. I'll wash everyone's clothes if that's what it takes to find Angela. I better go talk to Chris and see what he wants me to do." She turned to go, then stopped and looked back. "Nice job on the webcam thingy. You guys amaze me."

When he was alone, Tex pulled out his phone and looked at photos of his family, wondering once more if he had made the right decision to come here. He missed them so. It wouldn't hurt to call home a bit more.

***

Chris watched the screen as Liz walked into the laundromat. Tex watched her with binoculars. All three were wearing comm earpieces since the webcam didn't pick up sound.

"I bet she hugs the first person she sees," Tex said.

"I heard that." It was a rare softer version of Liz's voice.

They continued to watch as Liz walked up to one of the two women in the laundromat. "Excuse me. Do you speak English?"

"A little," the woman in the burqa said.

"Oh, good. I'm new here. I wonder if you could teach me how to wash clothes."

"Yes." she scanned Liz, up and down. "Uh . . . where are clothes?"

"Oh, I didn't bring them in yet. I work in that

bookmobile across the street. I wanted to find out if I need coins and soap and such. And then how to turn on the machine."

Liz's new friend looked out the front window toward the minibus and then back to Liz. "Okay. You watch me?"

"Yes. Show me."

The woman in the burqa opened the door of a washer and put clothes in. Then she went to a vending machine on the wall and showed Liz a coin.

"That's a euro, right?" Liz asked.

"Yes, one euro." She put the coin in a slot and selected a box of laundry detergent.

Liz nodded. "One euro for detergent."

Liz's teacher put the detergent in the machine and closed the door. Then she showed Liz two euros before placing them in slots above the washing machine.

"So," Liz said. "Two euros for washing machine. Now, what about the dryer?"

"Ah . . . dryer so, so. One coin, two coin, maybe three coin."

"Well, thank you," Liz said. She held out her arms, but seemed to hesitate. "You are so kind. Do you mind if I hug you?"

Chris turned to Tex. "That's a first."

"Yeah. Liz asking for a hug."

The burqa-clad woman looked stunned, but she seemed to move a micrometer toward her, all Liz needed to go in for the hug.

Once released from Liz's arms, the woman looked at her and waited. "Are you going to wash clothes now?"

"Oh, not today."

"Ah. I thought you may have clothes in that, what you call it?"

Chris made a guess. "I think she wants to see the bookmobile."

Liz cocked her head. "Bookmobile. Do you have time to look at the bookmobile?"

"Yes. Yes. May I?"

"Of course. That is why we're here. The books are in German mostly. Do you know German?"

"Only a little. I'm learning though."

"Well, come on, I'll show you the bookmobile."

Chris motioned Tex away from the window. "Better step away as they walk across the street. Liz's new friend may wonder who we are."

It wasn't long until Liz and the woman were no longer visible on the screen because they were outside the webcam's view. Chris and Tex could still hear everything they said however.

Liz was talking. "I am so glad you wanted to see the library. We only recently opened and you are our first visitor."

"First?" the woman said.

"Yes. Now, what kind of book are you looking for?" Liz asked.

"I cannot buy books today. Not enough money."

"Oh, the books are not for sale. You pick out what you want and take them. No charge. If you want to bring them back later, that is okay."

"If we're still here," Chris said softly, not wanting

to confuse Liz.

"I see," the woman said.

The bookmobile was quiet for a few minutes.

"I take this one."

"Good. All you need to do is put your name on this card to check out the book."

A few minutes later, Liz said into her comm. "The coast is clear. Did y'all hear. We had our first bookmobile customer."

"Congratulations," Chris said.

"Wonderful," Tex said.

"She took one of the Arabic language books Heinz bought for us. I'm not sure what it is about. Her name is Liliane something. I can't read her last name."

Heinz returned to the operations control center from yet another smoke break. "What is going on? I saw a woman in a burqa leaving the minibus. Is all good?"

"Everything is fine." Chris looked into the man's eyes wishing he could trust him. "Liz had her first patron. She checked out one of the Arabic books you provided. If that continues, we may need to buy more books."

"Why do we need the mobile library?" Heinz asked. "How is that helping find your wife?"

Chris thought they'd already discussed that. "The bookmobile gives us legitimacy, a reason to be parked in this large vehicle out in front of the refugee camp."

Heinz nodded slowly. "I suppose so."

The call from Volker came around 3:00 PM.

Chris gathered his friends. "Volker is meeting

Amin at the laundry at 4:00 PM today. Liz, why don't you go on over there now. Take your clothes and buy some detergent. Act like you do it every day. Try not to hug too many people, but be yourself. An American tourist in an odd place, but you won't need to explain why you're there. You can tell people about the bookmobile if you want to." He gave her a handful of coins.

Liz smiled. "Okay. I can do all that. But, why am I really there?"

"We want to see if the comm you're wearing will pick up the conversation between Volker and Amin. Volker said they speak German since he doesn't know Arabic. Heinz will be listening in and translating here at the control center."

Liz nodded. "So, you want me to get close enough to hear, so the comm can pick up the discussion?"

Chris nodded. "Yes."

"Perhaps," Tex said, "she should let them know she doesn't know German and they'll feel more at ease about her being able to hear them."

"Good idea," Chris said. "Liz, you might start up a conversation with another customer and be loud enough for all to hear."

She laughed. "I can do loud."

Chris studied her for a moment. "Do you feel safe doing this?"

"Sure," Liz said, standing tall with her arms folded.

"Good. I thought about sending Heinz or Tex in with you, but I think either one might scare Amin away. You'll be wearing the comm to pick up their conversation, but you can also use it to holler for help if anything goes wrong. We're not that far away."

She smiled. "I know. I'll be okay."

***

Angela stared at the closed door. The man unlocking the door knew her name, but he wasn't a friend. She looked at Emma and shook her head.

Reyaad Amin was the notorious ISIS recruiter she'd been searching for. He was the reason she'd been assigned to work with refugees in Germany.

Emma looked frightened.

How far could Angela go to protect this young opera singer? She needed to concentrate on protecting herself now, and her baby.

The door opened and Amin walked in alone. "Are you decent?" He laughed at his little joke, knowing it was too late to ask. His English was better than the others, but he had the same strong accent.

Once she saw him, she understood how he knew her name. She'd served on the same committee he had. He'd used a different name, but she'd never forget that face. It contained a six-inch scar that ran from below one eye to his neck. She knew it was the same man. The ISIS recruiter had worked with her on the committee and pretended to help the refugees find jobs while what he really wanted was more fighters and suicide bombers.

Amin looked only at Angela as he paced around the room while remaining as far away from her as possible. Angela moved also to stay between him and Emma. Angela didn't want a repeat of the way they had forced her to obey by holding a knife to Emma's neck.

He stopped. "So, Ms. Charlene Frank. We meet again. I assume you remember me, correct?"

Angela held visual contact. "I do. I hope you are staying busy helping the refugees find decent jobs. I'm afraid I haven't had the opportunity to help lately."

He laughed loudly. "That I am. I provide them wonderful jobs with many benefits."

Suddenly, his face took on a seriousness that changed his bearing. He crouched like a wrestler and stepped left then right with his arms held out as if he were going to grab her, grinning as he circled her.

She was ready to take him on and was disappointed when he backed away, straightened his body, and filled the room with laughter.

"Ha, ha. Fooled you. I heard you fight like a man so I wanted to see for myself. You fight me?"

"I don't fight like a man. I fight like a *woman*. And, no, I don't want to fight you. But, I will if it is necessary."

Amin nodded as his eyes smiled. "Yes. You are spy. Real women don't fight with men."

"Women fight in my country. Many of them take self-defense classes because scum like you try to take advantage of them."

The hand he'd waved in the air was pulled back and aimed at her face. He stopped himself before he touched her and laughed again. This time louder than before. "I want to teach you a lesson on how to be a real woman, but not today. There are more important things to take care of." He turned toward the door.

Angela didn't respond, but she was ready to defend herself and her unborn baby as well as Emma.

Amin left. Angela didn't move until she heard the door lock snap into place. What was that about? Clearly, he wanted her to know he recognized her from the job search committee, but why? What else did he know? Was he guessing she was a spy or did he have more information about her than he had just admitted? And, what about Emma? He'd ignored her. What was he planning for them?

CHAPTER SIXTEEN

Tex pushed his Stetson back and moved in for a closer look at the screen showing the camp. "Look. Someone's coming out of the locked room."

"It's a man. Not the usual older woman," Chris said.

Tex combed his hair back. "I'm sorry, but I didn't see him enter."

"I didn't see him go in either. I wonder if it's Amin. It's about the time he is supposed to meet Volker"

Tex nodded. "Probably him. Look, he's walking toward us."

Heinz pointed. "And now he is on the other screen walking toward the laundry. And there's Volker, too. Yes, it's him. Both men right on time."

Chris adjusted his earpiece. "Heinz, they're getting

ready to enter the laundry. Do you hear anything? If so, be ready to translate."

"Am hearing fine. But, only washer and dryer sounds. No talk yet."

"That's all I can hear," Chris said, "except for the music. Liz will do her best to get close enough for us to hear their conversation."

Heinz leaned toward Chris. "Are you sure you don't want me to go in there? That way I could listen and protect Liz."

"No. Don't worry about Liz," Chris said. "What she lacks in strength she makes up for in assertiveness."

Tex laughed. "That's right. She might give Amin a bear hug . . . and take his breath away."

"I heard that," Liz used her soft voice again.

Chris smiled. "Don't hug anyone, Liz."

"I won't. I'm not stupid."

Chris shook his head. "I know. Focus, everyone. We can see them through the window. Can anyone hear them?"

"I can." It was Liz's voice. "Sounds like German. Are you picking up anything, Heinz?"

"No. I can hear you, but not Volker and Amin. I should be there with Miss Liz."

"No," Chris said. "We don't want to expose you yet. Your German will come in handy later. If we don't hear anything today, it'll be okay. Volker will tell us what was said."

Chris watched the screen. Liz folded clothes without looking toward Amin and Volker.

Liz whispered, but what she said was clear to the

men in the minibus control section. "Heinz, you wouldn't be able to get closer anyway. They're over in the corner. Amin eyed me suspiciously until Volker moved, purposely blocking Amin's gaze. I better get busy with these clothes."

Liz's phone rang. She pulled it out and pressed the answer button. She didn't say anything.

Amin nodded his head toward the door. Volker followed him out.

When the two men were gone, Liz put the phone to her ear. Chris, Tex, and Heinz could hear only her end of the conversation. "Hello, Samuel? It's not really a good time. Can I call you right back?" She paused. "What? It may be urgent?" She turned off her comm.

***

When Liz got back to the minibus, all three of the men were waiting. Chris asked first. "Well, what did Samuel say? What might be urgent?"

"He wanted to let us know someone in a suit and tie showed up at the farm asking a bunch of questions about Angela and you. He told the stranger the truth. That he was Angela's uncle and was house sitting while the young folks were out of the county."

"Did that satisfy him?" Chris asked.

Liz shrugged. "Don't know. Samuel said the man drove off in a black Land Rover."

Tex pushed his hat up to expose his forehead, which he gave a vigorous rub. "Probably MI6 nosing around. If Samuel hadn't been there I bet they'd have gone in and sniffed around a bit more."

Chris nodded. "Probably. Or, they may have lost track of us since we left the Airport area and were checking to see if I was home." He looked at Heinz to get his reaction, but their interpreter stared straight ahead and didn't flinch.

"Could be," Liz said. "I still don't trust that Nathan character, even if he *is* Angela's partner."

Chris turned back to business. "Thank Samuel for us, Liz. For handling the situation the way he did and for letting us know about it so quickly. Now, what did we learn from the meeting between Amin and Volker?"

Liz spoke first. "We learned we should send Heinz if we want to understand a German conversation."

Tex puffed out his lips. "Hmm. Thinking outside the box, maybe we could put one of our comms on Volker and then we'd be able to listen in from a distance."

"Not a bad idea," Chris said. "I hope we find Angela quickly so we don't have to deal with listening to Amin and Volker."

"Besides," Liz said, "putting that loop thing on him could get him in bad trouble if Amin found out."

"Or, we could have sent me in," Heinz said with arms crossed.

Chris read Heinz's negative body language, but didn't let it daunt him. "That was my decision. I didn't want to expose you just yet. You'll be our ace in the hole. If we can't hear what Amin and Volker talk about, we can ask Volker later. I think he'll continue to cooperate with us for a few more euros. Liz said he tried to block Amin's view of her. That's an indication of Volker's support."

"What *did* we learn, Doc?" Tex asked.

"Two important things," Chris said. "First, we now know what Amin looks like. We can watch for him in other situations and places. Second, we know where he went right before meeting Volker. The door was locked on the outside which means he may store the materials he wants Volker to deliver."

"Or," Tex said, "he lives there and may have stopped by briefly to get something."

Chris nodded. "That's possible. We'll be able to determine that after watching that door for a while."

"Did you see him carrying anything when he came out of the building?" Liz asked.

Tex looked at Chris. They both shook their heads. "No," Tex said, "but he was wearing a coat and could have put envelopes or something small in his pockets."

Liz combed her hair with her hand. "I didn't see Amin give anything to Volker, but a transfer from one to the other could have been made during the time when Volker got between me and Amin." She turned to Chris. "That's something else to ask when you talk to Volker. Did Amin give him anything."

Chris nodded. "Good idea. We also have it all on video. We can replay it to see what else we can spot. One thing is sure, we should keep a close eye on that building. Tex, make a log of who comes and goes along with date and time. And keep the video camera working all night."

Liz scratched the back of her neck. "Does that

mean we're going leave the minibus here?"

"Yes," Chris said. "It's not far to the hotel. Everyone okay with walking back?"

Liz and Heinz went out the door and walked toward the hotel.

Tex pulled the lever to lower the lift and waved at Liz. "Meet y'all later."

Chris stared at the monitor showing the refugee camp door where Amin had stopped on his way to meet Volker.

"What's up?" Tex asked.

"I'm not sure. All I know is I want to get into that building, through the door Amin used. There's something crucial inside."

Tex watched the screen with Chris. "Are you thinking Angela could be held there?"

"No. that's doubtful. Unless she's bound, she could take that scrawny Amin guy. Or, she'd find a way to escape. No, I don't feel she's there. But, I think we'll find a clue to where she is in that building and I'm going to figure out a way to get in."

Tex nodded. "I have an idea. You asked me to log visitors. We can use that data to find the best time for us to break in."

"Right. The log not only tells us when people are going in and out, it also tells us when no one is there. Say, can you review the film from tonight when we get back here tomorrow while continuing to record?"

"Sure. I can view in fast forward mode so it doesn't take long."

"Good. Michael is studying the area and looking at

other possible places in the camp where they could be holding Angela."

Chris prepared the lift for Tex's use. "We better get going. The others are waiting for us. By the way, let's keep the log and the break-in plan to ourselves. No need to bother Liz and Heinz about it."

Chris noticed Tex's eyes pop over to his when he mentioned Heinz. "What's wrong with Heinz?"

"Probably nothing. I just don't want to alarm them."

***

The call from Michael came while Chris was alone, on his way to the restaurant to meet the others.

"I've got a little news for you alone. Okay to talk now?"

Chris felt his body tense. His intuition about people usually panned out and he was concerned about what to do if Heinz wasn't who he said. "Tell me."

"I found many Heinz Gabriels, and none matched the photo you sent."

"Nothing, then."

"Not quite. I was able to get into MI6's computer. The word Gabriel was mentioned in several places. It wasn't specific to you or Angela, but they were talking in general terms about him being in Berlin looking over the situation."

"Interesting. They could be talking about someone else, but it could be our man."

"Yes. It was like he was working for them, not you. How did you meet him?"

Chris remembered when they first met in the hotel lobby and he seemed to be the right person. But, no one ever checked his credentials or identification. "Supposedly, our benefactor's friends hired him. I'll have to check that out."

"Well, sorry, I couldn't learn more. I'll keep looking if you want, but it doesn't appear promising."

"No need. How are you doing on the other project?" Chris realized Nathan had the ability to bug his phone and wondered if he should be more careful.

"I'll have a report for you tomorrow."

"Good. Encrypt it, will you?"

"Sure."

***

Angela felt her muscles tighten from the sound of the door lock being manipulated. Emma, who had been resting on her bunk, sat up, fear creeping over the youthful innocence of her face. Angela could understand how the young woman could appeal to theatre-goers. Emma had a way of expressing her emotions with her body. Adding that to her singing ability made her all the more interesting as a performer. Right now, though, Emma looked like a child afraid she would be punished for something outside her control.

Angela quietly moved closer to the entryway, taking her usual position between the enemy and

Emma. This time the enemy was only Liliane bringing food and water. Angela relaxed and started to consider ways to take advantage of the unlocked door. She wouldn't bolt leaving Emma to face the wrath of ISIS. But she might look out and see what was going on in the real world.

Liliane placed the dusty canvas bag on Angela's bed and picked up the empty bag. "You eat."

Angela made her way to the door Liliane left unlocked during her short visits. As she walked slowly she thought of another weapon they could use. The empty canvas bag from the previous delivery could be thrown over Liliane's head. It would disorient her and muffle her screams long enough to tie her up with the electric wire Angela had stashed under her mattress.

Liliane turned toward the door where Angela stood. "No, no."

Angela laughed. "Don't worry. I'm only looking. You know I would not leave here. I love it here."

Liliane squinted and stared at Angela in disbelief. "Yes, yes. You stay."

"I want to see outside. It is so boring being inside all the time. Tell me what is happening in the real world." She wanted to learn more about her surroundings in case she had an opportunity to escape. Once before when Liliane let her look out, she'd noted the street and the laundry.

Today, a small bus was parked on the street. A passenger bus, but a special one. *Fahrbücherei*, it said. Mobile library. The thought of it took her breath away and reminded her of how Chris and his friends bought

SIDNEY W. FROST

a bookmobile in England when they were there looking for some guy who'd stolen money from Liz.

The question seemed to confuse Liliane. "Real world?"

The bookmobile gave Angela a sense of meaning and triggered her mind to consider an escape. She could use her electrical wire to tie Liliane up and make a run for it. They wouldn't have to go far to get to that mobile library.

Emma had been so negative and slow to react, she wouldn't be much help, but Angela couldn't leave her. If she did, Emma could become a sex slave to one of the ISIS generals and never be found again. Any plan for escape had to include a way to take Emma with her.

Liliane pulled Angela away from the door, warning her with an emphatic shake of her head. "No. Understand? Must not leave."

Liliane went out and shut the door behind her. The sound of the door being locked echoed in the room. It was too late to escape today.

Angela caught her breath as she realized the *Fahrbücherei* might be here for her. It would be like Chris to use it to rescue her. She laughed, reminding herself it was outrageous, perhaps a symptom of being held against her will too long. There was no way he could be in that bus. Still, the possibility of his nearness made her light-headed.

She opened the food bag and gave Emma her share. "Better eat. We need to keep up our strength."

Emma stared at the wall. "Why? So we'll look

more appealing to the rapists?"

***

After dinner, Chris pulled Tex aside and spoke to him privately. "Come with me to my room. I need to talk to you."

They told Liz and Heinz goodnight and went to Chris's room. Tex tossed his hat on the bed. "This is about Heinz, isn't it? I expected this conversation might come up. I've noticed you're not letting him do as much as you did at first. What's going on?"

"Have you noticed how he wants to be involved in everything? I appreciate the fact that he's willing to help, but we brought him on as an interpreter. I feel like he's studying everything we do. I hate to say this, but I keep thinking he's collecting information to share with someone somewhere."

Tex looked at Chris for a long time without responding. "He asks a lot a questions, doesn't he? But, I think he's just curious. He told us he has some experience as a private investigator, so he's not merely a translator."

"I began withholding information for fear he'd tell someone. Then I asked Michael if he could find out anything about him."

"And?"

"It's not definitive, but Michael found a reference to Gabriel in the MI6 files. He said it looked like Heinz is working for them."

"Why would MI6 want to spy on us?" Tex asked.

"All they have to do is ask and we'd tell them everything we know."

Chris shook his head. "I know, but something feels wrong about the way Heinz acts."

"We got him from Brian's friends. If you're uncomfortable with Heinz, call Brian and see if we can get someone else."

Chris took a few seconds to mull over the suggestions. "That's basically what Michael said. I'll call Brian right now. He might tell us not to worry about Heinz, that the man is simply that way."

He pulled out his phone and found Brian's number in his list of contacts. "Here, I'll put him on speaker so you can hear, too."

"Hello."

"Brian. This is Chris. Tex is with me and you're on speaker phone. We have a question for you."

"Okay. Everything all right there?"

"Yes. We're making some progress, but we haven't found her yet. My question is about Heinz."

"Heinz? Who's that?"

"You know. The interpreter your friends got for us."

The phone was silent.

"Brian, are you still there?"

"Yes. I'm here. But I'm afraid there's a problem. The interpreter my friends sent said he was dismissed and was told you decided you didn't need him."

Chris nodded. "We *do* have a problem. I was going to tell you the interpreter you sent has been too nosey and we were going to ask if he could be replaced. But now, I find we have a spy working for us."

Tex shook his head in disgust.

Brian continued. "Do you want me to call my friends and have them send the real interpreter back to see you?"

Chris looked at Tex before answering Brian. "No. Not yet. Let us deal with Heinz first and see what we can learn. Bringing a replacement would probably send Heinz into hiding. We want to find out who he's working for before we cut him loose. Maybe we should create some fake information, something so spectacular he'll have to report it immediately, and see what happens."

"I'll bet he's working for MI6," Brian said. "They probably sent him in to learn what you know. It's a compliment, really."

"Maybe, but I still don't like it. Okay, Brian. Thanks. That really helps. We'll get back to you if we need a real interpreter."

Chris hung up. He and Tex were silent for minutes before Tex spoke.

"So. What do we do now?"

A soft knock on the door sounded.

Chris walked toward the entryway. "Wonder who that could be this time of night."

Tex turned his wheelchair to face the door, and shrugged.

Chris opened the door to Heinz Gabriel who nearly filled the opening.

CHAPTER SEVENTEEN

Chris watched as a nervous man shifted his weight from one foot to the other, while he looked at the floor. "Hope I am not disturbing you at this hour, but is important we talk."

"Come in."

"Oh . . . Tex here too. Good. I need to talk to both."

"Have a seat." Chris pointed to the only chair in the room.

Heinz sat, stared at the floor and cleared his throat.

Chris helped him. "What's on your mind?"

The German looked up. "I am not person you think. I was hired by Nathan to work for you and tell him what you do."

Tex blared it out. "You're a spy for MI6?"

Heinz turned to Tex. "No. I am not spy. I am interpreter who was out of work and needing a job. Nathan and Angela hire me sometimes. I did not know they work for MI6. I was told you interfered with a government project and I should see what you do and tell Nathan."

"That's what a spy does," Tex said. "You're a plant, pretending to be on our team, but working for someone else."

Heinz looked at Chris. "I do not understand what that means. But, I came to say I must resign. I leave now."

Chris sat on the edge of the bed. "Do you mean you resign as our interpreter?"

"Yes. Also, I resign from Nathan."

"Why? You said you needed the work."

"I do. But, now I know you . . . " Heinz looked at Chris. "And Liz . . . " He smiled, but his eyes glistened. "Liz is nice lady. She hugs me every day. Never have I worked with anyone so kind. I feel awful for what I have done."

Tex rolled closer to Heinz. "So, why not stay?"

Heinz frowned. "How? I have betrayed you."

Tex reached over and patted Heinz on the arm. "We'll turn this around on Nathan. He made you a spy. We'll make you a double agent. You give him misleading information and tell us what he's doing."

Chris shook his head. "No. Let's not ask Heinz to do that. That's what's upsetting him, even if it would be turning the tables on Nathan. We should be working *with* MI6, not against them."

Chris faced Heinz. "But we can offer you a job. Go ahead and resign your job with Nathan. Stay with us and continue to help us. We'll continue to pay you as we agreed."

Heinz looked incredulous. "You would do that for me?" His eyes opened wide. "After what I did to you?"

Heinz reached into his pocket and brought out a wad of bills. "Here. This is yours."

"What is that?" Chris reached for the bills.

"The money you gave me to find Angela's room."

Chris pushed it back toward Heinz. "You can keep the money. You found her room number."

"No. I got it from Nathan. I didn't use the money for desk clerk. I lied to you."

Chris put the money in Heinz's hands. "That doesn't matter now."

Tex nodded. "Don't worry, Nathan will find another way to watch us. I'd love to have you spy on Nathan, but Chris is right. We shouldn't ask you to do that."

Heinz smiled. "I can work for you without reporting to Nathan? That is wonderful."

They all shook hands and Heinz walked toward the door. "Thank you, both. You will not regret this."

Chris placed a hand on Heinz's shoulder at the door. "We know. Back to work tomorrow."

"Yes," Heinz said as he left.

Chris sat on his bed and held his face in hands. After a few seconds of silence, Chris looked up. "Did we do the right thing?"

Tex nodded. "I think so. We could've told him we

already knew he was a phony and had pretty much guessed he was working for MI6."

"Yes, but there was no need to. What worries me, and tell me if I'm paranoid, is that MI6 bugged my room or my phone and they heard me talking to Brian."

Tex laughed, and picked up the story where Chris left off. "And then Nathan called Heinz and told him to come in here with some outlandish story about resigning. Yes. You're a bit paranoid. I'm not saying that couldn't happen. They are a spy organization with unlimited resources. They could be listening to us right at this moment talking about them bugging your phone. But, I doubt it. Heinz seemed sincere, and Nathan hasn't acted as if he is that concerned about us."

Chris looked around the room. "You're right. They could be listening right now . . . and laughing . . . but, I think we've done more to find Angela than they have."

"You're right. They'd be smart to monitor us and keep an eye on what we do."

Chris didn't respond right away. "All we have to do now is lead them to Angela."

"We will," Tex said.

Chris nodded. "We'd better get some sleep. I want to go through the video tomorrow and see if we can find anything useful."

Tex wheeled toward the door. "Okay. Goodnight, Chris." He raised his voice. "*And goodnight, Nathan.*" He laughed as he rolled out of the room.

Chris called to let Brian know about Heinz.

***

After breakfast the next day, Chris, Tex, and Heinz met in the control center to review the video of the room near the entrance to the refugee camp while Liz opened the bookmobile section to the public.

Tex monitored the real-time view of the door on one screen while Chris and Heinz looked at the video history on the other. A fast-forward review showed nothing. But when they got to the time right before they arrived this morning, a figure popped on the screen causing them to stop and rewind.

Heinz pointed at the screen. "Look. There is a woman in hijab at the door."

"Yes," Chris said. "She's carrying a cloth bag of some kind."

"Check the time stamp," Tex said.

Chris leaned in to better see the time stamp. "Seven thirty this morning."

They watched as the woman on the video unlocked the door and went in.

"She probably didn't stay long," Tex said. "She left the door cracked open."

Chris moved in to block his view. "Hey! Keep your eyes on the live action. Heinz and I can take care of this."

"Sorry. My view is boring."

"Yes, but we don't want to have to look at it twice. I'll tell you if there's something you need to see here. Interesting about her leaving the door open, though."

"Yes," Heinz said. "Tex must be correct. Must mean she won't stay long."

"Or, the door only locks from the outside." Chris said.

"Look. The woman is coming out." Heinz pointed toward the screen. "Wait, that is not same person. This one is shorter. Her head not covered. She just looks out, not leaves."

Chris wondered if it could be Angela.

"She is gone now," Heinz said. "I only saw side of her head."

They backed up the tape and reran it several times. But, Chris couldn't tell if it was Angela or not. "I can't see enough of her face. It could be her, though. Why would she peek out like that instead of making a run for it?"

Finally, Chris pressed play to move forward. "The woman in the hijab is coming out. And she's carrying the bag as if it's empty."

Heinz nodded. "I see what you mean. On way in she held bag upright. Now it hangs like empty."

***

The next day, while the woman in the hijab was there, Chris saw someone peek out. It was only a silhouette, but enough to let him know someone was in the room. A person who was locked in the room.

And Chris knew who it was. "She's in there. I know she is. Clearly, the old woman is delivering food and water to whoever is locked up inside."

"I don't know." Tex slowly shook his head. "If she can look out like that, why doesn't she run? Angela could outrun the old woman. What's keeping her there?"

"Maybe she is chained, or tied up."

Heinz's observation pained Chris. He considered the possibilities, but kept them to himself. "You're right, Tex. If it's Angela, she'd run if she could. We need to assume she's physically restrained in some way. The question is, what can we do to get her out of there?"

"Here's what we know." Chris grabbed a notepad and a pen, ready to make a list if that would help. "Other than the time Amin stopped by, no one has visited the room except the old woman in the hijab and she is there twice a day on a fairly predictable time schedule. Other than telling us it's probably a hostage situation, what else do we know?" He held the pen over the paper, waiting.

"That Angela is there and she cannot escape?" Heinz offered.

"Maybe." Chris wanted her to be there. If she was there, he could free her. "We can't say for sure it is Angela, but we can surmise *someone* is being held captive. Regular visits twice a day could be meals. But, what we know is there's a lot of time when no one is outside the door."

"That's right," Tex said. "Why can't we walk right up there right this minute and knock on the door? According to what we've seen, no one would be the wiser."

"That's true." Chris wanted to do just that, but he had to look at all possibilities. "But if we do that, we might blow our cover and lose all we've gained. I'm not ready to take that chance."

Heinz pointed at the image of the screen. "What could go wrong if we go to door and knock? If person challenges us, we can say have wrong place."

Chris leaned back in his chair. "For all we know, there's someone like us nearby with a webcam pointing at that door, and perhaps another pointing at us."

"Hmm, I see. If we can do, they can do."

"Yes," Chris said, "and if they spot us, everything changes. We could lose the advantage parking here affords us."

"Heinz," he asked, "does Nathan know about our vehicle and the webcam watching the door?"

Heinz looked down with a sheepish expression. "Yes. That was before, you know. I have not talked to him since I resigned. I promise."

"It's okay. I'm not accusing you of anything. All I want to know is what he knows."

"I told him, but he scoffed at information and said was, what was word, amateurish."

Chris made notes on his pad. "Okay, so MI6 may have eyes on the door, too. They could be looking down from a high-flying drone. I'm more concerned about what Amin is doing. Have we seen anything to indicate an alarm being set after the door is closed and locked?"

Tex viewed his live feedback screen. "You mean one that alerts someone elsewhere that the door was opened?"

"Yes," Chris said.

"No, I haven't seen anything, but it wouldn't take much. Home security systems do this with a piece of metal on one surface and a magnet on the other. An alarm sounds when the circuit passing from one to the other is broken. If they're using anything like that, it would have to be reset every time the old woman made her food delivery, assuming that's what she's doing. The resetting could be done remotely and we wouldn't see anything."

Chris added to his notes. "What do you two think about waiting until dark and going up to that door and knocking?"

"There's no need to wait," Tex said. "It doesn't get real dark there. We could easily be seen."

Chris studied the entrance to the locked room. "What if we took out the light above the door?"

"That would work," Tex said. "But it'd make it harder for us to see as well."

"We could use a flashlight." Chris added that to his list.

Heinz scratched his chin. "What if person in there is chained? She could not leave with us."

Tex rolled around to get closer to where Chris sat. "I know. We'll take a chain cutter, for the door lock and her chains. We could set her free in seconds and be gone before anyone has a chance to stop us."

It was clear to Chris they were referring to the hostage as female. Was it Angela? Were they that close to freeing her?

Chris shook his head, not in disagreement but because of the impact of what Tex had said. "Wait. Let's look at all that could go wrong if we do what you're suggesting."

"Like?" Tex asked.

"What if there's an alarm? Or, someone watching? What if she's not there? Breaking in may let Amin know we're here."

Tex scratched his head. "If an alarm goes off, we'll have to get in, grab her and get away before Amin and his thugs can react."

Chris considered possible scenarios as he checked his notes. "I think it's worth a try. Heinz, can you find a chain cutter and a flashlight? Something to break the lock on the door and snap a chain that may be holding someone in the room. And get a knife, too. She may be tied with rope."

"*Kettenschneider, Taschenlampe,* and *Messer.* Yes, yes, *natürlich.*" Heinz stood and pulled on his coat and walked toward the door. "I am back before dark."

While Heinz was gone, Chris received an encrypted message from Michael summarizing the Mitte camp and identifying places where prisoners could be held. Michael's analysis showed the room they planned to break into was the most likely place in the camp to hide someone.

CHAPTER EIGHTEEN

Angela told time, or approximated it, by the strip of light that sneaked in through a crack above their prison door. During one of her looks outside while Liliane was there, she'd seen a porch light that apparently stayed on day and night. With the door closed, sunlight was either white or grayish depending on the weather. At night, she surmised, when only the porch light showed, the light over the top of the door was yellow.

She was anxious to escape. Emma needed to be out of there. The young opera singer was sleeping more each day and eating less. She'd given up on washing her face and combing her hair. And she wasn't doing anything to stay healthy and strong. Angela had urged her to join in on a daily exercise routine, but Emma wasn't interested.

Angela knew these were all signs of depression, most likely caused by the woman losing control of her life.

The sound of the padlock opening caught Angela's attention as it always did. It had been several hours since the light over the door had turned from bright white to warm yellow. This was new. Who would be coming in at this time of day? Something was wrong.

She reached over the side of her bed and found the electrical wire she'd threaded through the springs, held her hand over the spot, ready to slide it out if needed, but careful not to expose it otherwise. She stood near her bed.

Liliane walked in with two men, one she hadn't met. The new one was Burhan, the guard Emma called "the nice one." The other one was Nizar, the one she called "the vulgar, ugly one." The fat vulgar one, Sayid, wasn't with them. Both men held guns in their hands and both rushed to a spot between Emma and Angela. They must have known Angela would protect the young singer.

"We come for girl." Liliane gestured toward Emma.

The girl they wanted was on her cot. She didn't move. Her eyes were closed. She couldn't have fallen asleep so fast. Angela had talked to her about her lack of exercise ten minutes ago. Was Emma aware of their visitors or that Liliane was talking about her? Was she pretending to be asleep?

"Why do you want her?" Angela asked as she

slowly shifted her position to get closer to her roommate.

She'd taken one step when Nizar moved into her pathway and nudged her with his gun.

Angela stopped her forward motion, but didn't retreat. "Why are you taking Emma?"

Emma looked up and frowned. "Take me? Who? Is Mommy here?" She looked around the room. "Mommy?"

Liliane moved to where Emma lay on her bed and grabbed one of her hands. "Come. We'll let you talk to your mother."

"Where are you taking her?" Angela surveyed the situation and moved closer to Emma.

The captors intervened once again, forcing her back toward her bed.

"Not your business." Liliane pulled Emma up and handed her a hijab. "Wear this."

Emma pulled away. "Why? Where are you taking me?"

Liliane continued to force Emma to her feet. "Don't worry. You won't be harmed. We need video. Something your people call *proof of life*."

Angela stiffened. That meant the abductors were trying to get a ransom for Emma, as she had suspected. She had also said her parents didn't have much money. The request for proof of life was usually a stalling technique.

Angela ignored the armed kidnappers. "What about me? Let me go with her to help. She's not feeling well."

Liliane laughed. "No one pay for you."

The older woman pushed Emma toward the door while the two men backed out of the room, keeping their guns trained on Angela. She heard the lock snap into place. She felt all alone, and, in a way, relieved.

***

"Liz, can you drive this vehicle?" Chris waved an arm indicating the minibus.

"Sure. I drove the British red double-decker bookmobile back home all the time before Michael joined me. And the Austin bookmobile before that. This should be simple compared to the double-decker which is bigger and taller."

Chris's beard felt too long and he tried to comb it with his fingers. At home, he kept it short by trimming it often. Being on the road had made that impossible.

"Good. I'd also like you to monitor the action on the screen while Heinz and I are breaking into the building. That way you can warn us if you see anyone coming our way."

Liz shook her head rapidly. "Oh . . . no, no, no. You know I don't get along with computers. They hate me and never do what I want. Can't Tex do it?"

"I've got another job for Tex and it involves him being outside."

"Do I have to do the computer thing?"

Chris laughed. "All you have to do is look at the screen and tell me if you see anyone moving toward the locked room. It's more like watching TV than using a computer. But, if you like, I can ask Michael to help do it. Two sets of eyes will be better anyway."

"Oh. Could you? I could probably do it without him, but don't ask me to touch the keyboard thingy or the mouse thingy. Every time I touch something on a computer it goes wacky."

"Sure. I'll contact him."

Liz gave Chris a hug, his second for the day.

"And, pardon my saying so, Tex, but I'd like Liz to help you get back onboard as quickly as possible. We may have to leave here in a hurry."

Tex laughed. "I won't need any help. Besides, she can't make that lift move any faster than it does."

Chris ignored him. "Heinz, you and I will go to the room and break in. I'll unscrew the outside light while you break the lock. If there is anyone in the room, we'll take them with us back to the minibus."

"What if we do not find your wife?" Heinz said.

"Doesn't matter. Someone is being held against their will. Whoever we find, we take with us when we leave. If it's not Angela, we'll turn them over to the police."

Tex twisted his wheelchair and moved toward the lift. "What about me? What do you want me to do?"

"Take your pistol and park your wheelchair on the sidewalk that leads to the camp entrance. There is a rock wall there about three feet high. It will only partially protect you from gunfire. If we must leave in a hurry, cover us. When the prisoner is safe, I'll cover you while you get back to the minibus and inside as fast as you can with Liz's help. If Liz is at the wheel, we'll all help."

Tex nodded. "Got it."

Chris looked at each person, waited for any questions. "Okay. It's as dark as it's going to get. Let's do this."

"Uh-oh." Tex pointed to the monitor. "Someone else got there first."

Everyone looked at the screen. Three people were outside the building. It looked like the old woman who they usually saw during daylight hours. With her were two men. They appeared to have guns drawn as they shoved open the door.

Even on a good day, Chris couldn't stand change. He had a fear of the unexpected and his stomach churned now that everything seemed to be going wrong. In all the time they'd been watching, no one had ever come at night. Why were they there now? The presence of armed guards might indicate they were going to move the prisoner.

This could be the last chance to rescue Angela. But only if they moved in a hurry. Chris was ready to go and he only hesitated because he didn't want to put his friends in harm's way. Before this change, there was possible danger. Now, the threat was real. The danger was definite.

Tex looked up at Chris. "Whadda you think? Should we go after them? Two are armed. We can take them out if we have to."

Chris finally decided. "No. These are people who cut off heads and shoot women and children. We can't risk it. Let's wait and watch. Then we can make a better decision."

They didn't have to wait long. The old woman came out first pulling someone in a hijab. Right behind them were the two guards. They locked the door before the four of them walked toward the camp.

Heinz turned to Chris. "Was that your wife they took?"

"I don't think so. I couldn't see her face. But the way she walked and carried her body makes me think it wasn't. Also, some blonde hair poked out. It couldn't be Angela unless they made her wear a blonde wig."

Tex nodded. "I agree. But, what do we do now? Were we wrong to think Angela was being held there? Has this been a wild-goose chase from the start?"

"I hope not," Chris said. "But, I'm beginning to think she's not here after all."

Liz cleared her throat the way she often did before speaking. "There's one way to find out, and I believe we're all ready to do it."

Chris looked around and smiled when everyone nodded. "Let's go then."

In a matter of minutes, everyone was in position. Chris stayed onboard until Liz parked the minibus as close to the building as possible and left the motor running. She moved to the control center to watch the action on the computer screen and shrugged.

"You don't have to do anything but look at the screen and let us know if anything unexpected happens. We moved the lens that was pointed toward the laundry to show a wider area of the camp entrance. Michael is standing by if any software changes are required."

"I'm here," Michael said over the comm.

"Thank you, Michael," Liz said. "Good luck all, and be safe." She gave Chris, Tex, and Heinz a quick hug.

Tex positioned himself halfway between the minibus and the locked room. He parked his wheelchair on the sidewalk near the rock wall, gun in his lap.

Chris and Heinz walked quietly to the locked door. Chris reached up and turned the porch light bulb enough for the light to go out. He knocked softly. "Anyone there?"

No response. "Cut it open."

He held the flashlight while Heinz used the new chain cutter to snap the lock into two pieces.

Chris pulled the door open. The room was dark. "Anyone there?" he asked again.

"Chris?" Angela whispered as she rushed into his arms. "I can't believe you're here."

His body quivered with relief. "It's me. We need to cut your chains so we can go. They may be back soon."

"I'm not chained."

He had trouble understanding, but it wasn't the right time to ask her why she hadn't escaped. "Okay. Let's go."

"No." She pushed away. "I can't leave. But I'm glad you're here. I need to get a message to MI6. Talk to my partner, a guy named Nathan. . . "

He pulled her toward the door. "I've met Nathan. You can tell him yourself. He's probably in town."

Angela held back. "You don't understand. Listen.

There's not much time. Memorize this. Tell Nathan to find Reyaad Amin. He's the kidnapper. They have Emma McCleary, the missing American opera singer."

"Please come." He took her by the arm and walked toward the exit.

"No. Listen to me. You must get this information to Nathan. Tell him to warn the Americans not to pay the ransom. If they do, I'm dead and Emma will be sent to the ISIS front line as a sex slave. The ransom money will be used for weapons. Tell him also I think they suspect I'm an agent."

"Then come with me now. We have a vehicle waiting." He pulled her out the door and pointed to the bookmobile.

She pulled back. "I can't leave Emma."

"We'll get her later."

"No. She'll never make it without me. Please, there isn't time to explain it all. Leave now before it's too late."

He grabbed her and pulled her out of the room. "I can't let you stay."

She pleaded with her eyes as she jerked away.

Chris heard Liz's voice. "Look out! They're headed your way."

A gun fired. Chris and Angela both crouched on the porch. It sounded like the slug hit the building near where they stood. He saw several men moving toward them from the camp's main entrance. He aimed his pistol toward the men.

Before he pulled the trigger, he heard Tex's weapon sound and saw one of them fall. "Hurry," he said to Angela, "Run to the bookmobile while Tex covers us. Heinz, are you there? We've got to go."

He pointed his Glock toward the captors, but Angela pushed his arm down. "No. You might hit Emma. See, they're hiding behind her. Go. I'll be okay. I love you." She pushed him away from the door.

Chris didn't move. "No. We came to get you. Once you're free, you can set Emma free."

Angela shook her head. "It'll be too late. We'll never find her if I leave now."

"I don't care. We can make it, but we've got to move now."

"Go without me, please."

One of the kidnappers suddenly moved in closer to where they were and aimed his gun at Chris. Angela used what looked like electrical wire like a whip and managed to wrap it around the man's arm. She jerked it right at the time he pulled the trigger.

The blast missed Chris but he felt the concussion as he hit the floor with his weapon aimed at the man.

The kidnapper screamed as he freed his arm from the wire and this time aimed at Angela. Chris aimed at the man and pulled the trigger. Blast! The guard dropped his gun and fell to the ground.

Chris reached for Angela to take her to the bus, when another guard appeared, got behind Angela. One hand held her by the hair while the other hand pressed a knife to her throat. He flashed a demonic grin, showing gaps where his front teeth should be. "What now?"

Another captor held the other young woman in a

similar position.

He could shoot either one without hurting the hostage, but he couldn't shoot *both* in time to save the women.

"Wait," Angela said loud enough for all to hear. "I'll go with you, but let my friends leave. Chris, Tex, hold your fire, please."

Heinz was on the ground, not moving. Tex was bleeding near his right shoulder. The minibus had gone over the curb onto the sidewalk and was sitting a few feet from where they were standing. Liz poked her head out the window and nodded her head toward the door.

Chris turned back toward Angela, hoping to free her from the knife-wielding man, but she was gone. So was the other woman and the one holding her. Even the guard he'd shot, the one who had fallen to the ground, had disappeared. He surveyed the area and saw Volker's van driving across the field, running through fences and speeding away.

CHAPTER NINETEEN

Chris's first thought was to jump in the minibus and follow Volker's van. Angela was in that van and he had to catch up to her before it was too late, before the van was out of reach.

He fought the urge to immediately go in pursuit.

How could he? His friend Tex was bleeding and Heinz was unconscious. He couldn't leave them on the street to face the police who would surely be arriving soon. Even if he tried to follow, he had no idea which way the van had gone.

The chase was over. The rescue had failed.

He stopped the negative thoughts as soon as he recognized them. He wouldn't accept failure.

Instantly, his mind churned with possible strategies for finding and rescuing Angela. One thing was for sure, he'd never give up.

He walked over to Tex and examined his friend's wound through the torn shirt. Chris could see a two-inch slice on the shoulder. Blood oozed out of the jagged cut. "It looks like the bullet cut into your shoulder and passed on through. It is serious, though. All we can do is stop the bleeding. You're going to need some stiches."

"It's not so bad, Doc. I'm sorry we didn't free Angela. I'll be okay. You should go after that van before it gets too far away."

"We'll catch up to them soon enough. Right now, I want to be sure you're okay." Chris helped Tex remove the shirt. "We'll get you some help. In the meantime, hold the shirt on the wound to stop the bleeding I need to check on Heinz."

Tex held it against his shoulder. "I'm all right. The bullet barely grazed me. "

Chris turned to Liz, who was hanging out of the driver's window. "There's a first-aid kit on the dash between the front seats. Bring it and see if you can help Tex. I don't know what happened to Heinz."

"Shouldn't you go after Angela?" Liz asked.

"Can't. Not until we take care of Tex and Heinz."

Liz nodded. A few seconds later she ran out of the minibus, first-aid kit in hand. She went to Tex. "Where'd you get hit?"

Tex held his shirt away from his shoulder. "See, I'm okay. It's not even bleeding now. Y'all help Heinz first."

Chris knelt over Heinz. "I can't see any blood. "

Liz joined Chris, and checked Heinz's pulse. "Praise the Lord. He's alive."

Heinz groaned and tried to get up as if to prove he was indeed alive. "What happened?"

"That's what I was going to ask you," Chris said, as he and Liz helped the man into a sitting position. "One minute you're snapping the lock on the door and the next you're flat out on the ground."

Heinz rubbed the back of his head. "Ouch. Someone must have hit me from behind."

"Liz, watch Heinz. Probably a concussion so he should stay awake. I'll put a bandage on Tex."

Chris dug through the first-aid kit and found what he needed. He pulled out antibacterial cream, a gauze bandage and tape to hold it in place. "All right, Tex, let's fix you up."

Tex smiled. "If I'd got this wound in the marines, it'd mean a Purple Heart. Always wanted one of those. Only thing I got was a Good Conduct medal."

Chris went back to Heinz and looked into his eyes. "Heinz, are you feeling well enough to do something for me?"

"Yes. What can I do?"

"The police will most likely be here soon. Angela gave me a message for Nathan and I don't want to get held up by the police. I don't even know if these guns are legal for us to have."

Heinz sat a little straighter. "You want me to call Nathan?"

"Yes. Tell him our situation and let him know we need assistance quickly."

"Yes." Heinz reached for his phone.

"Stress how we need help with the local cops. And tell him we have an important message from Angela. That should get him here in a hurry."

Chris helped Heinz stand. "In the meantime, let's get everyone into the minibus. Hopefully, Nathan can ease the situation with the police, but let's not muddy the water with these guns out in the open."

Heinz looked at Chris. "Muddy water?"

"Never mind," Chris said. "Call Nathan, please."

Liz pushed Tex's wheelchair toward the minibus. "Y'all know I'm against guns, period. But I have to admit they may have come in handy this time."

Chris thought of ways to respond, but nothing seemed important now but to find Angela.

"Michael," Chris all but whispered over the comm. "We need another plan. Start thinking."

"Will do."

***

Nathan arrived before the police got there, but only barely. He and two other men talked to the local law enforcement officers while Chris and the squad waited in the minibus.

Nathan and his two friends in suits showed the police what looked like ID's. After a few minutes of discussion, the police walked to their squad cars and drove away.

When the police were out of sight, Nathan entered the minibus control center. "Fancy set-up you have here." His gaze landed on Tex's bloody shirt. "You okay? We can get an ambulance if needed."

Chris answered for Tex. "Gunshot. Shallow. We put some antibacterial cream on it and bandaged it. A larger bandage would be nice, and ... perhaps someone to see if he needs stitches. The wound is ragged, and a little deeper than it looks."

"I don't need no stitches. It's not bleeding anymore." Tex pulled back his shirt to show no new blood had seeped out of the bandage Chris had applied.

Nathan nodded and leaned out the door where the two men in suits waited. "We need a medic."

One of them climbed in and looked around. Liz hugged him.

"All I need is a larger bandage," Tex said.

Chris could see this delaying the search longer. He wouldn't have called on Nathan to help if Tex and Heinz hadn't needed medical assistance. Chris didn't want all these government types to slow him down. He needed to find Angela. The trail was cold, but he'd find her . . . somehow. The van was on the run and the watch . . . .

Nathan looked around. "We can take care of that and get our MD to look at it. Anyone else hurt?"

Chris pointed at Heinz. "He got a bad bump on his head and was out for few minutes. Seems okay now, but I'd feel better if we could get him checked with an MRI. I don't want to go to a local hospital and explain what happened, though."

Nathan turned to man in the suit. "What do you

think, Rick?"

"No need for a hospital. We've got an emergency room on board our plane, including an MD and MRI unit."

Everyone seemed to be moving in slow motion. Chris couldn't hold back any longer. "Nathan, we're losing valuable time. You probably know we got here tracking Angela's watch and we can still find them. But only if we move quickly. Can your friends take Tex and Heinz to see the doctor so we can try to pick up the trail?"

Nathan didn't hesitate. "Sure. Rick, will you or Jake drive this bus to the plane with Tex and Heinz? Liz, you want to go with them or ride with us?"

She didn't take time to think about it. "The boys will be okay. I'll go with you and help any way I can."

Rick leaned out the door. "Jake, come on in. You drive this vehicle to the plane and ask Nolan to look these guys over. Heinz needs an MRI for concussion. Tex has a gunshot wound on the right shoulder."

Once Jake was inside, Rick continued. "The rest of us will go look for the kidnappers and meet you back at the plane. What are we looking for?"

"A GPS watch in a van," Chris said. "The kidnappers left in a dark van belonging to a German named Volker Dohr. He seems to be a legitimate businessman. We don't think he even knows Amin is a terrorist. He may or may not have been forced to help them get away or they may have stolen his vehicle.

"One of the terrorists was shot, maybe two. Volker was wearing a GPS watch that belonged to Angela.

He'd gotten it from Amin. We paid him to give the watch back to Angela if he got the chance."

Jake walked to the driver's seat and got hugged on the way.

Chris grabbed his laptop and pistol, gave a quick glance toward the squad, and walked out with Nathan and Rick.

Nathan drove while Rick sat in the back with Liz. Chris took the passenger seat so he could navigate. However, it turned out, he didn't need to.

Chris opened his laptop and brought up the tracking program, logged in and waited. Soon, a glowing dot appeared on the screen. It wasn't moving. Had they stopped for gas already? Had they reached their destination? He looked at the time. It'd been a little over an hour since the van left the area. Something was wrong.

"So?" Nathan asked. "Where are they?"

Chris enlarged the map display to read the street names around where the computer was showing the watch to be. "Hmm. This is strange. The watch appears to be in the warehouse where we think Angela was originally held. Where you found the RFID chip." Nathan grimaced and looked away.

"Perhaps they didn't make a run for it after all," Nathan said. "Maybe they went back to their old hiding place to throw us off. You said one or two of their people had been shot. They may need time to recover before making a run for it."

Chris wished he was driving. "Doesn't matter why. Let's go look. You remember how to get there?"

"Of course."

"Then let's hurry."

"Who are your American friends?" Chris asked, now that they were on the road heading toward where the watch was located.

"Sorry, we haven't had time to meet. I'm Rick Tisdale."

Chris reached over the seat and held the man's hand briefly without shaking it. "Nice to meet you. Chris McCowan. The lovely lady next to you is Liz Helmsley."

"Jake and I are FBI. We're here looking for a missing opera singer. A US citizen. We were meeting with Nathan when your SOS came in."

"The missing singer, is her name Emma?"

The agent's mouth popped open. "Yes. Have you seen her?"

"No . . . maybe. She wasn't there when we made the rescue attempt, but earlier someone in a hijab we'd not seen before showed up on our surveillance camera being taken away."

"Could it have been Angela?" Nathan asked.

"No. Different body type. Plus, we saw some blonde hair peeking out."

"Why do you think it was Emma?" Rick said.

"Because Angela told me to tell Nathan that an American opera singer named Emma McCleary was with her. She also said don't pay the ransom. If you do, they'll kill Angela and make Emma a sex slave.

"Also, when we went in for the rescue, Angela wouldn't let me shoot because she said two of the terrorists were hiding behind Emma. But it all happened so quickly, I wouldn't know her if I saw her again."

Chris looked at the speedometer. "Do you want me to drive?"

Nathan frowned. "No. I've got it."

He sped up some, but not enough for Chris.

"Who's Angela again?" Rick asked.

"My partner. The one I told you about." Nathan slowed for a turn, and glanced at Chris as he sped up again.

"Oh, she's MI6," the FBI agent said.

"And Chris's wife," Liz said.

"I see. What else did Angela say about McCleary?"

Chris paused, then turned to where he could see Rick and Liz in the back seat. He remembered it all, but he sorted through the information to find what might help the FBI the most. If they found the opera singer, his wife would be with her.

"It's not so much what she said, but what she did. Angela had a chance to escape and wouldn't. Emma had been taken somewhere and Angela was there alone when we broke in. I did everything in my power to force her into the minibus, but she refused because she was worried about what might happen to the opera singer if Angela left her alone."

Nathan nodded. "So, she felt she had to be there to protect Emma. Anything else?"

"Yes. She thinks they suspect she's an agent and to find Reyaad Amin. He is the one holding her and Emma." Chris turned his gaze to Nathan. "Does that name mean anything to you?"

Nathan shook his head slowly, not to say no, but to show his frustration. "It means he'll be hard to find."

"*We* found him," Chris said.

Nathan frowned and spoke louder. "Yes. And now, because of you, he's on the run. I know enough about him to know we'll never see him again. He's probably on his way to Syria right now."

Rick shook his head. "Nathan, I'm sensing some negative vibes here we don't need. Let's let these civilians help. They seem to be the only ones making any progress. Didn't you say you didn't know anything about where Angela was until today? And, isn't this the first lead anyone has had on the whereabouts of Emma McCleary? I, for one, am extremely appreciative for it."

"We would have found Angela, Emma, too, but now they're gone again. And, the kidnappers know we're looking for them." Nathan's response made him sound like a spoiled child who'd been told to play nice.

Rick nodded. "I'm sure you would've located her on your own, sooner or later, but rather than dwelling on the past let's see what we can do to rescue Angela and Emma."

"We may look like amateurs," Liz said. "But, we're not. And we've got a letter from the President of the United States to prove it."

Rick looked at Chris. "So, you're *that* Chris McCowan. I thought your name sounded familiar." He reached over and gave Chris another handshake, this time a little more vigorously. "Nice to meet you. Heard all about you—from your dad."

"You've worked with my dad?"

"Several times. When we need a computer specialist, we always call him first."

Computer specialist? Chris wondered if that's what they called white-hat hackers now.

Rick looked at Liz and stared at her for a second. "Say, you must be the hugging librarian. I've heard of you, too."

Liz smiled. "I hope what you heard was nice."

"You're the one who found a bunch of stolen antiquities in Texas, right?"

Liz nodded. "That's right. The FBI helped return them to the churches from where they had been stolen."

"I'm honored to meet you, ma'am."

"We're here and I don't see any vehicles," Nathan said. "The place is deserted. What does that laptop of yours say, Chris?"

Chris looked at the screen and checked. "It's dead. No internet service. But this must be the place. Pull over here. See the large door there. The van could be parked inside."

CHAPTER TWENTY

Nathan parked in front of the warehouse where they'd found Angela's RFID chip.

Chris closed his laptop and dropped it on the seat as he climbed out of the vehicle. Memories of the place caused him to take a deep breath. This was where Nathan had hidden Angela's clothing from him and hadn't bothered to tell Chris about the evidence she'd been there. Nathan claimed he did so to keep from hurting Chris, but it only made things worse.

Everyone got out and looked around. It was quiet. Unlike the Mitte camp, no stores were open, no cars drove by, and no one walked the streets.

Rick turned to Chris. "Before we go in, tell us what we might expect inside."

Chris appreciated Rick's question and the

professional way he treated the Vengeance Squad. "We aren't sure how many ISIS personnel there are. Probably four males and one female. The woman seemed to be controlling the opera singer. One of the men was shot and was on the ground. However, he was gone when I looked a few seconds later. Or, it might have been minutes. I don't know if he got up on his own or was carried away by his friends. Another one may have been shot, but he retreated. Everything happened fast and I was more concerned about Angela than anything else.

"In addition, we might encounter Volker, the driver, inside. If so, we should assume he is being held against his will and we should keep him safe. There could be five or six people watching three. Angela, Emma, and Volker."

"What do you know about this group of terrorists?" Rick asked Nathan.

"Amin, the leader, is the ISIS recruiter we came to Germany to find. We don't know the others, but we assumed he wouldn't be working alone. Angela told Chris Amin might suspect she's an agent. She didn't say why she thought that. She may have had to expose her ability to defend herself. That would certainly have made Amin suspect her of being more than the job counselor she claimed to be."

Chris added his thought about what happened. "Or, they may have discovered the RFID chip and left it to throw us off. In fact, we think finding the chip is what spooked them and caused them to move to the Mitte Camp."

Rick turned to Chris. "And the driver, how will we know which one he is?"

Chris answered. "He's German. All the other men are Middle Eastern."

Chris walked toward the warehouse door, the same one he'd entered days before when he tracked Angela's RFID chip. "I wish we could see inside before we open that door, it'd give us an edge. We used to have a beetle drone, but someone stepped on it."

Nathan jerked around. "I didn't know it was one of yours."

"Now, boys," Liz said. "We were going to work together."

Rick shook his head.

"Too bad we didn't come in the minibus," Chris said. "We've got some more beetle drones plus some other electronics that would help us check out the inside of the building before going in."

"Yeah, *we* could've brought some surveillance gear also." Rick said. "But, here we are. We've gotta work with what we have. When we left Mitte Camp, the watch was inside this building. Let's go in and look for it. If it's not there, then they've had even more time to get away. Everyone agree?"

Nathan pulled out his gun. "Liz, would you wait in the car? I don't want any friendly fire incidents. Remember, we've got three hostages to protect."

Liz got back in the car.

Chris remembered something. "Michael? Are you there?"

Rick looked puzzled. "Michael? Who's Michael? You

got a comm piece on?"

"He does," Liz said through the car window. "Michael's my grandson in Texas."

"Michael, we're getting ready to go in. Would you verify the GPS watch is still in the warehouse?"

"Sure. Hang on."

A few seconds passed before he responded. "Yep. Hasn't moved since you left Mitte Camp."

Chris repeated what Michael said for Rick and Nathan. "Thanks, Michael. I don't like the fact that the watch hasn't moved, but at least we know it's there. We're going in and when we do, let us know immediately if that watch moves."

"Will do."

Rick held his pistol high, opened the warehouse door slowly, and entered the building. Nathan and Chris followed.

They spread out and moved in cautiously.

Nathan found the watch. "Over here."

The watch was on Volker's wrist exactly where Chris thought it would be. Unfortunately, Volker's lifeless body was on the floor surrounded by more blood than Chris had ever seen in one place. There was a hole in the man's head and his hand, the one with the GPS watch on it had been severed and was a few feet from the rest of his body.

Chris whispered so Michael and the others would know. "Watch is here. Volker's dead."

Rick looked at Nathan. "No sense checking for a pulse. No one could survive this. Want to call it in? Or, would you prefer I do?"

"You can. I think the government here trusts Washington a little more than they do London. Plus, I called in the last one."

Rick nodded and pulled out his phone.

Chris pointed at the watch. "Okay if I take this? It was my wife's."

"Sure," Rick said.

Chris unfastened the watch to remove it so he wouldn't have to pull it over the bloody stump.

***

After the local police got to the warehouse and Rick explained the situation to them with a great show of ID cards, the squad drove to the airport to meet the others.

The FBI plane was in a remote part of the regional airport, away from the terminal and curious eyes of baggage and fuel handlers. The plane was so large it made the bookmobile parked nearby look like a toy.

Chris was torn. He wanted to see what the plane looked like inside, but he didn't want to waste time. He had to find Angela. The next time he found her, he'd take her away from her captors, no matter what she said.

Chris's memory and his love of military aircraft led him to identify the FBI plane as a Lockheed C-130 Hercules with a ramp large enough to accommodate a full-sized automobile.

A good relationship with the FBI could help find Angela faster. Since they were searching for Emma and

Angela wanted to stay with the singer, then the only way to free his wife might be by finding Emma. It wouldn't hurt to get to know these FBI agents a little more.

He decided to check the plane quickly to see how Tex and Heinz were doing, and to see if they could go with him to rescue Angela.

He followed the others up the ramp. When they got up closer to the belly of the plane, a jeep and a black Chevy Suburban were parked at the top of the ramp. Beyond the vehicles was a door held open by Rick.

Inside the room was a control center similar the one in the minibus, only much larger. A huge desk was in the center of the room with computers at each of six workstations. On the wall was a world map with a row of clocks above the various time zones. There was no one in the room and the computers were silent.

They kept walking.

The next room reminded Chris of a ship's galley with stainless steel tables and chairs bolted to the floor to prevent movement during flight.

Chris smelled fresh coffee and his desire for a cup almost overwhelmed him. But, He resisted. There wasn't much time.

Liz walked swiftly toward the coffee service and grabbed a mug. "This is what I need."

"Help yourself," Rick said. "Anyone else want a cup?"

"Do you have tea?" Nathan asked.

Rick pulled out another mug. "Sure. Bags here, hot

water there."

"How about you, Chris?"

"No thanks. I want to check on the guys." He also wanted to get started with his new plan. The only thing he cared about was finding Angela. Being here, talking to these government types only slowed him from completing the task.

Rick walked toward another door. "Follow me. I'll show you where they are."

Liz took a gulp of coffee and put her mug in the metal sink. "Hey, I want to go, too."

What Chris saw in the next room reminded him of a hospital emergency room. There were four beds and all types and shapes of electronic medical monitoring equipment. Unlike the ones found in hospitals, the beds as well as the equipment were bolted to the floor.

Tex sat in his wheelchair next to one bed wearing a blue tee shirt with FBI in gold letters. Liz went to him and gave him a hug. "I prayed for you, Percy."

Heinz sat on the edge of a second bed. A woman in desert camo scrubs with a stethoscope around her neck stood beside him looking at a digital tablet. When she saw Chris, she lowered the device and introduced herself. "Hi. I'm Dr. Polly Nolan. You must be Chris and Liz."

Liz gave Polly a big hug.

"How's he doing, Doc?" Chris asked, nodding toward Heinz.

Nolan spoke to Heinz while answering Chris's question. "Mild concussion. You need to take it easy the next few days. If you're dizzy, no driving. Also, these things tend to be cumulative. Be careful not to bang your head again. And tell your doctor about this incident if you do."

Chris started to say, "We—"

"I know. You guys are in the business of banging heads. Just saying."

Chris smiled, but didn't tell her how tame and sedate their lives usually were. He patted Heinz on the back.

"Heinz is our interpreter," Chris said to the doctor. He then turned to Heinz. "Ready to get back out there?"

Heinz stood. "Ja. I'm ready." He wobbled some when he took a step, which made him look like he wasn't as ready to go as he thought.

Chris grabbed an arm. "Steady."

Heinz held on to the bed railing and closed his eyes. After a few seconds, he looked around. "Had to let the world settle down first."

"The dizziness should go away in a few hours," Doctor Nolan said. "You'll want to stay in bed, but it's best to get up. Do it carefully, though."

Chris kept his hold on Heinz. "There's no hurry. Take it slow and easy until the dizziness goes away."

Liz held his other arm. "Yes. Slow and easy."

Heinz squinted and looked around. "Okay. Maybe sit a minute." He sat on the edge of the bed. Liz stood next to him.

"Heinz, why don't you take off a couple of days. You deserve it after being knocked out like that."

"Oh, no. I will be fine. Doctor said to be awake."

"Yes, but if you are dizzy, you shouldn't be too active." Chris was concerned that Heinz might need more time to relax.

"I want to go with you." Heinz stood as if to show he was ready.

Chris walked to where Tex sat in his wheelchair and put an arm around his friend. "And what about this one, Doc. Is he ready to send back to the front?"

She started to laugh, but stopped quickly. "This one needs a purple heart. He told me all about his Marine Corps career and how he lived on the streets until he sobered up and reenlisted after 9/11 only to be paralyzed in a car crash caused by a drunk driver."

Chris was familiar with the story, and the irony of it. "How serious is his wound?"

Dr. Nolan smiled. "It could have been worse. We found evidence that makes us think the bullet hit the arm of his wheelchair first and then ricocheted. Shrapnel entered his right shoulder with enough impact to cut a slice a quarter of an inch deep and two inches long. I used ten stitches to close it, but he's going to be fine."

"Thanks, Doctor," Tex said and he started rolling toward the door.

Nolan looked at Chris. "Now, let's check you out."

Chris's eyebrows tightened. "Me? I wasn't hit. I didn't get hurt at all."

"Not all wounds are to the body. I understand you had to shoot one of the ISIS terrorists. Based on what I've heard and the amount of blood that was found at the scene, there is a good chance the man died if he didn't get immediate medical care."

Chris stared at the FBI doctor. "I guess."

"In our business, we usually counsel agents who have had to kill someone in the line of duty. I'd like to talk to you about what happened. We can do that privately." She motioned toward a door.

He thought for a moment she was kidding, but when she started to escort him out, away from the others, he knew she was serious. He held his ground. "That won't be necessary."

Tex spun around and rolled up closer to Chris. "Yeah, Doc, besides being a crack shot, he has nerves of steel."

Rick walked in before Nolan had a chance to argue her case. "Chris, will you follow me? There's someone who wants to talk to you."

CHAPTER TWENTY-ONE

Rick led Chris back to the control center. This time, one of the workstations was lit up and Chris saw why he had been summoned.

"Sit here." Rick smiled as he pointed to a chair facing the monitor.

From where he sat he could see his video image in the bottom left of the screen next to full-screen video images of his mother and dad.

"What are you doing in Berlin?" his mother asked without so much as a hello or how are you.

"Now, dear," his father said, "remember, Chris's friend Brian Donelson called and told us why Chris had to go to Germany. The main thing now is to tell him we love him and that we hope he resolves the problem of Angela's disappearance quickly and with her safe return."

"Thanks, Dad." Chris glanced around the room and saw Rick had left him alone to talk to his parents. "I don't know how secure this line is, but I'll call you when I can. Mom, I'm sorry if I upset you. I asked Brian to call you because it's difficult for me to talk about."

She leaned in closer to the screen. "I can understand you being upset, but surely you can talk to your own mother. Even when you're upset."

"I'm sorry. I'm not sure why the FBI chose to get you involved while the case is still unresolved. I can say we're progressing." He decided not to tell them about Tex's gunshot wound and the man Chris had to shoot and possibly killed. "Everyone is okay. We saw Angela and she hasn't been harmed. She could've gotten away, but she chose to stay to protect another hostage."

"Oh, my," his mother said.

His dad nodded. "You don't have to tell us more. We only wanted to see you and know you're okay. And to tell you how sorry we are about Angela. We understand why you don't have time to talk."

His mother leaned in again. "Yes. And we love you. Be very, very careful, son."

His dad smiled at his mother then turned back to Chris. "Just so you know, Rick is one you can trust. He and I work together occasionally. He travels a lot and I help him with some foreign computers . . . if you know what I mean."

"I know what you mean," his mother said, "and I

want you both to stop it. There's no need to put yourselves into such dangerous situations. Why can't you both teach like you studied to do?"

"I don't see anything wrong with Chris and I using our talents to help the government," his father said. "But, I'm concerned about you working on the investigation to find Angela. You're too close to the situation to be the one doing the investigation. Your chance of making mistakes increases when you're involved with the person in trouble.

"If you were a surgeon and your wife needed an operation, would you do it? No. You'd find the best doctor available and you'd stay in the waiting room. What you should do now is let the FBI and MI6 take care of this."

His mother chimed in. "He's right. You're too emotionally involved."

"That's true for most people," Chris said. "But you both know me well enough to know I can separate those things."

"I'm not sure that's still true," his dad said. "You used to be like a robot. But ever since you married you've changed. You're like the rest of us now. Think about it, son, and you'll know what I'm talking about."

"He's right, dear. Let the professionals do their jobs."

Chris wanted to tell them about the things he could do that the professionals couldn't. How he could access government computers without anyone knowing. As he thought about it, the germ of an idea that had been plaguing him suddenly erupted and he saw a solution.

He had to find that van—and Angela. That meant he had to break into the German traffic system. He could do that from the minibus in less time than the FBI and MI6 could get permission from the Germans to do so. He'd have to hurry though. There was no guarantee how long the van would be used. He needed to get to the minibus. Now.

"Okay, Mom. I'll let the FBI and MI6 do their job. Still, I want to be here when they find her. I'll stay behind the scenes and help only if they ask me to. Okay?" This was the only area of his life where he found it necessary to lie to his mother. He justified it by telling himself it would keep her from worrying about him so much.

"Talk to Rick, son," his dad said. "Remember what I said. You can trust him."

For a second Chris wondered if Rick had called his parents for the sole reason of getting him off the case. Could he trust the FBI? Should he tell them what he planned to do next.

He wasn't so sure about Nathan and MI6 after the way they had failed to help him find Angela. With Angela's well-being at stake, Chris would do whatever it took to get her home safely. Even lie to his parents. "Okay, Dad. I better get back to the hotel. We have early plans for tomorrow. I love you both."

Chris clicked the close button and the screen went dark.

Rick was waiting on the other side of the door. "Everything okay?"

Chris looked at him a few extra seconds. "Dad said I can trust you."

Rick nodded slowly, then handed Chris a business card. "This is for close friends only. Call anytime."

Chris looked at the card, then handed it back to Rick. "Thanks. I may take you up on that offer."

Rick looked shocked at getting the business card back.

"Don't worry," Chris said. "I memorized it."

Rick nodded. "Oh, yeah. I heard about that amazing memory of yours."

Chris found Liz in the ER and pulled her aside. "Get Tex and Heinz, say goodbye to our hosts, and meet me at the minibus. I have a plan bubbling in my brain and I want to get to the computer and try it before it's too late. We've got to find that van today."

He didn't explain or offer a reason for hurrying, but he knew Amin was smart enough to get rid of the van before anyone had a chance to find it and connect him to the death of Volker.

Liz pulled him in for a hug. "I didn't get a chance to say earlier, but I was sorry to hear Volker was dead. I know you must be concerned about losing him as a source of information. I've been praying for you . . . and dear Angela. Oh, and Volker's loved ones."

Chris held on to Liz a little longer than he usually did, nodded silently and then gently pushed away. He had initially been devastated when they found Volker's body, but hadn't shown those feelings. That was one of the advantages he had over others, his ability to suppress emotions. But he hadn't felt bad for long.

Now he had a new plan and was anxious to get started. He said nothing to Liz about it. He didn't want to say anything until they were alone, away from the FBI and MI6. He'd have to tell the government agencies eventually, but he felt it best to put it off as long as possible. He wanted to get out of here and find his wife without being hampered by government rules and regulations and country-to-country protocols.

He left Liz to round up the squad while he went to the minibus to get started designing a new app.

***

Chris was at the computer typing at full speed when the rest of the gang arrived.

Tex rolled off the lift and into place at the computer next to Chris. "What's the plan, Doc?"

Chris kept typing. "It might be too late, but I've hacked into the national traffic speed control computer. Michael wrote an app to track a license plate through the system."

Liz looked over his shoulder. "I'm so happy Michael is working with us this time. But, I don't understand anything you said, Chris."

Heinz answered before Chris had a chance. "It is a good plan. To control speeding. We have more traffic cameras in Deutschland than rest of EU countries combined."

"That's what I've read," Chris said. "And I've found where they store the information."

Tex pushed his hat to the back of his head. "How's

it work?"

Chris paused his typing. "It's simple. They photograph all license plates and clock the speed. If the vehicle is speeding, the owner is mailed a ticket."

"Yikes," Liz said. "Doesn't that mess up their insurance rates?"

"No." Heinz said. "Not like in America. We pay the fine and insurance stays the same."

"Okay," Tex said, "but how does hacking into the system help us? We don't know Volker's license plate number."

Chris smiled. "Sure we do. I memorized it when we first met Volker."

"The eidetic memory saves the day. . . again."

"Uh . . . I guess. That's not important. Here's how the license plate number is going to help us find Angela. Michael's app searches the files for Volker's van. Every time the plate number is spotted, a flag marks the location on a map. As soon as we have at least two hits, we'll move the same direction the van is going. Then, as new data points come in, we continue to follow. The app will post the route on our screen and overlay it on a map of the country."

Chris turned back to the screen and pressed some keys then stood and faced Tex. "I'll drive and you can watch the screen. As you discover changes in what the van is doing, call them out to me over the comm."

Tex moved in closer to the desk. "What do I do?"

"We have one hit on the map indicated by the red blinking light." Chris rose and headed toward the front of the minibus. "Let me know when you have a second hit."

Tex called out. "Wait. Is that all?"

"That's it."

Liz followed Chris to the driver's seat. "Hey. You had anything to eat lately?"

He wondered about her question for a few seconds. "I guess not, but we need to get on the road."

She pulled a sandwich out of her purse. "Here, try this. The rest of us ate on the plane. I saved this for you."

He looked at her. "Thanks."

Chris climbed into the driver's seat and unwrapped the sandwich. After the first bite, he knew it had been a long time since he'd eaten. With his unusual memory, he was amazed every time he forgot the simple things in life like eating but remembered most of everything he'd ever read. He finished the sandwich and took the soda Liz handed him before starting the motor.

Tex's voice came over the comm. "Three hits! The program works! The car was spotted on Bundesautobahn 11."

"Liz, check that map and help me get to A11."

"Will do."

Tex called out again. "Van is now on Bundesautobahn 20."

"Got that Liz? As soon as we get on A11, watch for A20."

Liz sat on the passenger seat near Chris and studied the map. "Here's 11 now."

Chris took the on ramp and gradually increased

speed while checking the gauges. He wondered if there'd been any damage to the bottom of the minibus when Liz drove up on the sidewalk to protect them during the rescue attempt. Too late to worry about that now.

Liz shut the map. "Looks like we stay on this highway for about an hour before we turn off onto 20. Think we'll catch up to them?"

Chris wondered how long it would take to do so. The fact that they were still getting hits was a good sign. He'd be surprised, though, if the terrorists didn't get rid of the van soon. He checked the fuel gauge and was pleased to see it showed full. "I don't know if we can get to them before they ditch their vehicle, but this is the only lead we have. I know you've been praying, but this would be a good time for a little extra."

"Will do." Liz smiled.

***

Angela watched as the van rolled on its side, bouncing as it went toward the rocky seashore below. It tumbled, bumped on several overhangs and bounced once at the bottom before settling upside down on a pile of water-worn rocks. It was so far from where they stood the vehicle looked more like a toy than a full-sized van.

The only one in the van was Burhan, and he was dead before the van was pushed over the cliff. He'd been shot during the rescue attempt at the Mitte Refugee camp and had died in Angela's arms during the drive from Berlin. She'd stopped the bleeding, but he needed more help than she could offer. She'd urged Amin to stop at the nearest hospital, but he'd refused.

Too bad Volker hadn't been with them. If he had, and had been wearing her GPS watch, Chris and MI6 would be able to find them. Now, she couldn't think of any way for Chris and the Vengeance Squad to know where she was. Even if Chris somehow found the direction the van travelled, it wouldn't be long before Amin would drive them away in a different vehicle.

Angela couldn't hold back tears, and that scared her. It had never happened before and she had to consider it was because she was pregnant. She wished she had gone with Chris when she had the opportunity. Wanting to protect Emma was automatic, based on hours and hours of training. The one thing she hadn't take into consideration was the baby. Chris's baby. She asked for God's protection for Chris and his friends.

Standing on the edge of the cliffs, she looked around to get her bearings. When this was over, she'd tell the authorities where to find Burhan's body. He'd been the only one who'd been nice to Emma, now the woman didn't act as if she knew he had died.

Angela didn't know exactly where they were. The last road sign she'd seen was for Jasmund National Park. At some point along the way, she'd heard them discussing a boat, but there was disagreement about where the boat was docked.

Emma stood next to Angela and had held her hand from the time the vehicle was rolled over the side by Amin, Nizar, Sayid, and Liliane. The young opera singer squeezed Angela's hand a little tighter now.

"Are we going to die?" Emma asked.

"No. They would've left us in the van if they wanted to kill us. No, I think they want to make some money off our kidnapping."

"Then why are you crying?"

Angela thought what best to say. "One of the men who tried to rescue us is my husband."

"What? Was he shot?"

"No. He got away. He'll be back for me. He's persistent. That's for sure."

"But how will he find us?"

"I don't know. But he will." That made her smile for the first time in a long while.

CHAPTER TWENTY-TWO

Two and a half hours later, Chris's hope of finding the van had diminished. According to the traffic control system, the van turned off A20 onto E251 toward Stralsund. No more hits had come in for the past half hour.

Now that the minibus was at the location where the van had been spotted last, Chris didn't know where to look or where to go next. Did that mean the van stopped in Stralsund? Or did it mean the traffic control system ended there.

Liz looked at Chris. "What do we do now?"

Chris looked around. It was a town on the water. Hundreds of boats were moored in the area. He continued to drive in the same direction as before. Only now he followed his intuition, not blips on a computer screen.

The road led them to a bridge. He slowed. "Check the map, Liz, and tell me what's up ahead. What's on the other end of this bridge?"

"It looks like an island. Small. This is the only road. If this is the way they traveled, we can't miss them."

"You're right. But that's assuming they crossed the bridge. We don't know that for sure."

Liz shrugged. "We've got to keep looking."

"Anything on the map, Tex?" Chris asked.

"Sorry. Nothing is happening."

Chris grabbed his phone and called Michael. "We're not seeing any movement on that van we were following. You see anything else in the Traffic System we can use?"

"Yes. I've got some information for you that might help. Since you followed the van into an area without cameras, I started searching emergency radio traffic in the area to see if the license plate showed up. It did. The fire department reported a van went off the cliffs not far from where you are now."

"The cliffs in Jasmund National Park?" Chris asked.

"Yes. That's it. My German is rusty, but I got the main words."

"Thanks, Michael. That's exactly what we needed. Stay on the phone, if you can. I'll add you to the comm loop. We might need your help."

Chris pulled into a parking lot to look at the map, but before he had time to stop, several emergency vehicles raced by with sirens blaring the way only

European vehicles could.

He hesitated. When he looked, he saw Liz's eyes locked on his.

"Is that the answer to prayer?" she asked.

"Prayer and your grandson's insights."

They followed the emergency vehicles, moving the minibus faster than they ever had before.

Tex rolled into the front. "Hey. Where we going?"

Chris sped up more. "Michael said the van went over a cliff. Let's pray Angela wasn't in it."

Liz nodded.

***

The convoy of emergency vehicles along with one bulky, lumbering bookmobile stopped at Jasmund National Park. Chris managed to pull in near the emergency vehicles before police set up barricades.

He waited until the rescue workers deployed and established a make-shift command center before he exited the bookmobile. "What's going on?" he asked.

"Who are you?" The man wore a dark blue uniform with *Feuerwehr* in bright yellow, along with several yellow reflective stripes. A white helmet sat on a portable table next to a large plastic-covered map.

"I . . . uh . . . " Chris was tired and hungry, but that was no excuse for sounding like an idiot. He needed to know what had happened and whether the rescue teams were here because of something that involved Angela or not. If not, then Chris wanted to know quickly so he could leave and re-start his search.

"Speak up, sir." The man sounded irritated.

"I'm worried about my wife." Chris blurted it out.

The man looked down at his map. "Sorry. This is an emergency rescue operation. Please go. You should call the police if your wife is missing."

"I followed a van she was in going this direction. Can you tell me if your emergency involves a van? I need to make sure she's okay."

The man looked up as if he noticed Chris for the first time. "A van?"

"Yes. It's a work-type van, with no windows in the back. An old vehicle, rusty, originally black."

"Why would your wife be in the van? Was she running away from you?"

"Oh, no. Nothing like that." He wondered how much to say.

"Look. We have work to do. All we know is that someone saw a vehicle go over the cliffs. I don't know what kind of vehicle it is. It could be a van, but it's a long way down to where it landed. So, excuse me. I have to get a helicopter out here to help." He picked up a phone and turned away from Chris.

"She was kidnapped." He said it quickly before the man had time to make the call."

The man lowered the phone. "She what?"

"She was taken against her will."

"Did you call the police?"

"Uh . . . not exactly."

"What does that mean? It's yes or no."

"I've been working with the FBI and MI6."

The German firefighter didn't laugh, but the look

on his face made Chris think he might. "Really? The American FBI, I take it?"

"Yes."

"And the British MI6?"

"Yes. My wife works for MI6."

The firefighter nodded a little longer than usual then grinned. "I see. And why would the FBI be in Germany?"

"They're here looking for an American opera singer who lives in Lűbeck, Germany. She went missing in Berlin." He knew it all sounded so lame. The German would think he was out of his mind. He searched for something to say to convince the firefighter he was not some kook or crazy person.

"An opera singer? Pardon. An *American* opera singer. From Lűbeck." Then he laughed as if relieved he wouldn't have to deal with Chris anymore since he had to be insane to come up with such a preposterous idea. "You've been reading too many spy novels. Get out of here. I've got work to do."

"It's all true." Chris pulled out a hotel note pad and wrote Rick's phone number on it and handed it to the man. "Call this number and they'll verify what I'm saying."

Chris suspected it was curiosity that caused the firefighter to call the number. After he'd asked a few questions, he looked at Chris and nodded several times before he handed him the phone. "He wants to talk to you."

Chris placed the phone to his ear. "Yes?"

Rick skipped to the nitty gritty. "What's going on?

Why are you interested in a vehicle falling off a cliff?"

"We followed Volker's van here."

"How did you do that?"

Chris heard the irritation in Rick's voice and wanted to explain. But he didn't want to take time doing it. He didn't care if the call upset Rick or not. His only concern was to find Angela. If it was, indeed, Volker's van at the bottom of the cliffs, Chris's mind raced through various scenarios of how the van got there and where the van's occupants were now.

He needed to verify the identity of the van, and its contents, before moving on to the next clue, if there was to be one. "Rick. I'm sorry I can't take time to explain. Tell this guy I'm legit so I can continue my search for Angela." He paused remembering why Rick was in Germany. "And Emma."

"I could help you more if you'd keep us in the loop."

"At first there was nothing to share with you. We followed a hunch. We did some things you couldn't have done due to your need to follow protocols."

"What things?"

"Do you really want to know?"

"Yes. So I can determine what to tell the firefighter."

Chris wondered if that was true, but he decided it didn't matter as long as what Rick told the man helped Chris search for his wife. "Nothing serious. We hacked into the government's speeding ticket system and found where the van had been. We lost it here at the Jasmund National Park.

"We had given up and started back to the Autobahn. Then, a bunch of emergency rescue units showed up so we followed them. I still don't know if the van we were following was involved. I need to get close enough to see."

Rick paused. "Okay. I'll make some calls to clear the way for you and then we'll join you. We'll be there ASAP."

"Thanks." Chris handed the phone to the officer, but they both turned their attention to the man being hauled up the side of the cliff.

"One dead in a van," the man in the harness called out. "No other bodies." He spoke German, but Chris understood every word.

"Man or woman?" Chris asked.

The harnessed man looked to the firefighter Chris had been talking to.

"It's okay. Male or female?"

"Male."

Chris took a deep breath. It was almost as if Angela had been rescued. She was still missing, still in danger, but she wasn't for sure dead in a rusted-out van at the bottom of a cliff in Germany. He exhaled and thanked God.

***

Angela and Emma sat on the ground behind a row of large rocks their arms tied in back, not far from Amin and Liliane, both of whom glanced toward them frequently.

Angela twisted slowly until she could see between the boulders. It wasn't long before Chris came into her view. He wouldn't be alone. She looked around the area and spotted the minibus.

She wondered how he'd tracked them to this remote location. It didn't matter. She needed to find a way to go to him, signal him, let him know where she was.

He was talking to a man in reflective firefighter gear, most likely a rescue specialist called in because of the van. Near the edge of the cliff they lowered a harnessed man over the side. He'd find the body. A male, he'd say, and Chris would know it wasn't her.

What would Chris do next? Where would he look? Would he find her in time? The other terrorists had gone to steal another vehicle. They'd be back soon and take her and Emma on the road again. She couldn't let that happen.

She looked at Amin. What would *he* do next? Since leaving Berlin he'd been irritable. Maybe mentally ill. At best a desperate and angry man about to lose control. As soon as he saw the cliffs, he had become more agitated.

With Sayid and Nizar gone for transportation, Amin and Liliane were the only ones to watch the prisoners. This was the best time to escape. That was imperative. She'd overheard Amin saying they may have to eliminate Angela and Emma. Amin had said the ransom money he could get for the women could buy weapons, but he was getting tired of babysitting. He wanted to get back to Syria and the fighting. The women were slowing him down.

Angela felt escape might work now because of the firefighters nearby plus Chris and his mates. Still, she knew if Amin was threatened, he wouldn't hesitate to kill them.

She worked her way over to Emma. "There's something I must tell you." Angela's voice was a mere whisper. She hardly moved her lips in case anyone was watching.

Emma didn't react.

Angela tried again. "Are you okay?" It was going to be difficult to rescue Emma without her cooperation.

Angela's hands were tied behind her, but she leaned on Emma's shoulder and bumped her gently until she looked up.

Emma opened her eyes. "What?"

Angela glanced at Amin and Liliane. "Speak softly and listen carefully. We can get away while the other guards are gone." Angela looked at their captors. Both continued to stare at the rescuers on the edge of the cliff near where the van had gone over.

"Are you listening?" Angela whispered.

Emma nodded, without looking at her.

"I'm a special agent from London sent here to investigate Amin and his associates."

Emma turned slowly toward Angela, her eyes widened. "You are?"

"Yes. And we've got to get away from them. They plan to kill us soon. With all the firefighters in the area, we can escape. Plus, my friends are here, too."

"Friends? Where?"

"See that minibus? They are in there and they'll help as soon as they know we are here."

"Minibus?" Emma looked over the rock she'd been leaning against. "I see it. Your friends are in the minibus."

Emma sounded strange, almost robotic. She might slow Angela's attempt to escape, but they had to try. Now. Before the other two guards got back. She moved her mouth close to Emma's ear. "See that man talking to the firefighter?"

Emma nodded.

"That's my husband. He's a computer specialist and I'd be willing to bet he has everything he needs in that bus to set us free."

Emma nodded, eyes wide open.

"As soon as he walks toward the minibus, be ready to go. When he gets about halfway there, we'll run toward it. Amin will be surprised and slow to react. By the time he figures out what's happening, Chris will see us and protect us."

"Okay," Emma said, nodding. "Escape. Run. Minibus."

"Yes. Be ready to move when I give the signal."

Emma stood. That was a good sign. She was preparing to run on Angela's signal. Or was she?

Something was wrong. Emma walked to Amin and whispered in his ear. He looked shocked then ran to Angela and grabbed her by the rope holding her hands behind her back, cinching it to make sure it was tight.

She looked down the hill. Chris was still talking to

the rescuer. What had Emma done? Was she one of them? Was all this a setup from the beginning? She remembered how she had not gone with Chris in Berlin when she had the chance because she wanted to rescue Emma. Was Emma part of the enemy all along?

"She's going to yell," Emma said.

Amin stuffed a foul-smelling handkerchief into Angela's mouth.

Had Emma snapped? It happened before. Stockholm syndrome they called it, where a captured person sympathized with the captors over time.

Amin motioned to Liliane. "Watch her."

When Liliane was in position near Angela, he handed the older woman a knife. "Kill her if she tries anything."

"No." Emma was emphatic. "We can't hurt her."

Amin looked stunned, but only for a nanosecond. He jerked his head toward Emma. "Kill her, too."

Emma looked different. Unafraid. No longer the victim, she was a woman with a purpose. "Hold her for ransom," she said, indicating Angela.

Amin's attention grew. "Her? Ransom? I can't even negotiate a ransom for a young girl like you, you stupid pig. Your parents can't get the money together. Besides, we can't do anything until Nizar and Sayid get back with a car so we can get out of here."

Emma laughed. "We can take that minibus."

Angela couldn't believe her ears. Emma was telling Amin everything.

Amin looked. "What minibus?"

Emma indicated the direction. "Right over there.

Doesn't it look familiar?"

"Hmm." Amin squinted. "That's the same one we saw at the camp. The one that almost ran me over."

"Right. And we need to get there now. Before her husband gets back."

"Husband?" Amin's eyes glowed with pleasure. "Liliane, cut this one free." He indicated Emma. "I like this one."

He laughed so loud Angela looked to see if Chris might have heard him.

CHAPTER TWENTY-THREE

As Chris walked back to the minibus, he wished he'd taken Heinz with him to help talk to the firefighter. He opened the back door. "Hey. Everyone okay . . . "

His friends were all there, but they were not alone.

He took in the scene before him. Liz was in the driver's seat with Tex and his wheelchair blocking her in. Amin held a gun to Tex's head. Heinz was on the floor, face down, arms tied behind his back. He peeked up at Chris, his eyes pleading for help or forgiveness or both.

Chris turned to the right and spotted Angela. The sight of her took his breath away. Her blouse was covered with blood, but her eyes told him it wasn't hers. He wanted to ignore the gun Amin held and the rest of the chaos in the minibus and rush to his wife and take her in his arms. But the thought passed when it registered on him the female captor held a knife to Angela's neck. There was a cloth in Angela's mouth and the angle of her arms hinted her hands were tied behind her.

Chris glanced around the area and didn't see any other ISIS personnel. Only Amin and a female with a knife. His gaze stopped on her a little longer than the other people and he noticed she looked as frightened as those being held prisoner. He also noticed she looked familiar.

He turned to Liz. She nodded. He realized the knife-wielding woman was Liliane, the one who helped Liz with the laundromat and then visited the bookmobile.

A young woman stood between Amin and the female guard. She moved freely. She had to be the missing opera singer. Why was she not tied up?

Amin spoke first. "Be very careful, husband of Charlene. What you do next will decide the outcome for all these lovely people." He moved his gun around, pausing as he pointed it toward Liz. "I'll shoot the old lady first and still have time put a bullet in your wife's lovely head, if Liliane hasn't killed her already with her trusty blade." He paused, a silly grin on his face.

Chris continued to survey the area for options.

Amin moved the pistol to where he had it aimed at Chris. "Now. If you want your friends and wife to live, you will drive us . . . "

"No." It was Emma. Chris was right. Something was wrong about her. Not only was she free, she was talking back to Amin.

His eyes opened wide and his body moved backward slightly. He was probably livid that a woman would talk to him in that way. He slowly turned the gun toward Emma, and paused as if waiting for an explanation before he shot her.

Chris wanted to take advantage of the shift in the gun's aim, but before he could, Emma continued.

She smiled and shook her head as if explaining a simple subject to a child. "What we need is money for the Jihad. You've tried for weeks to get my parents to pay up, and you should know by now that's not going to work. They don't have that kind of money. Besides, you don't need it. You have a prisoner who can get us some *big* money."

Amin looked at each person ending with Emma.

Emma nodded toward Angela. "She was sent here from London. She told me herself. Her job was to follow you. She's an agent. Her government will do anything to get her released unharmed. She's valuable." Emma smiled again and looked at Amin with her hands on her hips with smugness that said she expected his praise for a job well done.

Amin's scowl melted into a partial smile as he seemingly considered what Emma said. "But, how? We don't know how to contact them and we're not in a position to do much here with all the government rescuers hanging around out there. "

He turned to Chris. "You drive us now."

Emma nodded toward Chris. "He can get the money. Charlene said her husband is a computer specialist. Apparently, he can reach anyone in the world with a computer."

"So?"

Amin wasn't connecting the dots, but Chris knew where Emma was going. Was she an opera singer or an ISIS sympathizer?

Emma looked frustrated the way one does at times when people don't hear what was being said. "Think! You have a bank account somewhere, I presume." It wasn't a question.

Amin said, "Yes, but—"

"Then tell this computer expert to transfer five million dollars to your account. We don't care where he gets the money as long as it goes into your account, right?"

Michael's voice spoke softly through the comm. "I'm here. Use me."

Amin finally understood and his face lit up. "Right." He pointed his pistol toward Tex and looked around the area before he reached into his pocket and retrieved a folded letter-sized paper. "Here. This is number for a bank account in Qatar. When I see that the money is there, you will all be released. Except this blonde girl. I want her to be on my staff."

Emma smiled and nodded. "Thank you, sir."

Amin sneered, looking at her body instead of her face. "Yes. You will make a wonderful bride for one of my generals."

Emma's eyes opened wider and she gulped.

Chris crossed his arms. "No."

"No?" Amin looked surprised. "What do you

mean? You must. You have no choice. Get us the money or I kill your wife then I kill your friends and then you."

"Don't worry. I'll get you the five million, but only if Emma is freed also."

"You bargain for this silly blonde girl? Why do you care what happens to her?"

"She's an American."

Amin was silent, as if thinking.

Chris upped the ante. "Tell you what. I'll get you an extra million and we get Emma."

Amin was clearly happy about the monetary part of the offer, but he made a counter proposal. "Plus, a million for Burhan's family."

Chris looked puzzled. "Who's Burhan?"

"My friend. The one you shot and killed at the Mitte Camp." Amin clipped the words.

Chris didn't change his expression. "Okay. Seven million. We all go free. Deal?"

Amin evidently didn't want to show how pleased he was, but it came out anyway, though his attempt to hold back a smile turned it into a grin.

Emma wasn't happy. "I want to go with *you*." She indicated Amin. "And not as someone's wife. I want to be a fighter. Or a leader. Make *me* a general."

He slapped her face hard enough to knock her to the floor where she landed next to Heinz. "Stupid girl. She thinks she can be a general."

Amin looked at Chris. "Yes. Deal. And hurry. Nobody goes free until the money is in my account. I can verify it was deposited with my mobile." He handed Chris the paper with the bank account information on it.

Chris looked at the paper and read it aloud.

"Got it," Michael said.

Chris didn't move.

Amin looked shocked. "What's the matter?"

"Before I start I want that dirty rag out of her mouth." He indicated Angela even though everyone knew who he was talking about.

Amin looked as if he might decline, but instead, made a silent sign of assent to Liliane who pulled the handkerchief from Angela's mouth and pushed it toward Amin.

Amin shook his head and Liliane dropped it on the floor and wiped her hand on her burqa.

"Wow, Amin's Qatar account already has three-million US dollars in it." Michael's words went through the comm and Chris could see by their faces that Liz and Tex had heard everything he'd said.

Chris pulled the keyboard toward him, adjusted the monitor and reached for the mouse. "Now, all I have to do is find seven million dollars."

"Correct," Amin said. "And if you use that machine to contact anyone to come help you escape, guess who dies first?" He turned the gun until it was pointed toward Angela and said, "Pow!"

Chris blocked out the world. He typed, studied, typed more. "Hmm . . . here is a possibility. Account number is . . . " He spoke Rick's phone number instead of a bank account number.

"I'll call that number unless you say no," Michael

said.

"Yes, this looks like a maybe. I can get two-plus million from here . . . "

"Take it," Amin said.

"No. We may only get one chance before triggering some cyber cops. If we do, we'll get shut out with nothing. I need to get the whole seven million from one place. It is a huge amount so it will take time. Ah . . . this looks promising." He hadn't found anything. He was stalling, hoping he could come up with an idea to turn the tide.

Rick was already on the way, but now Michael could tell the agent what to expect when he got here. Stalling seemed the only way to get out of danger. All he had to do was dangle more and more money in front of Amin to keep the terrorist's eyes off what was happening.

Amin moved closer to the computer, where he could look over Chris's shoulder. "Hurry. We need to get out of here."

"I'm going as fast as I can." He brought up screen after screen of numbers, some decimal, but mostly binary. He continued to type gibberish while grabbing a look around the minibus as he did. When his eyes locked onto Tex's, his friend made a subtle head motion toward an open drawer nearby.

What was Tex trying to say? What was in the drawer that would help them get away? It was where they stored their guns. Was Tex going to grab a pistol and shoot Amin or Liliane before they could harm Angela?

That didn't sound logical. What else was in the drawer? Then he remembered. That was where they stored the small beetle drones. That was it! Chris nodded at Tex and turned back to the computer.

Amin was still looking over his shoulder.

Chris stopped what he was doing. "I can't work with you standing there. Look at the screen and you can see there's nothing that's suspicious."

Amin took one more look before he moved back toward where Tex and Liz sat, stepping over Emma and Heinz as he did.

Liliane still held the knife near Angela's neck.

While Amin's back was to Chris, Chris activated the drone program and flew a beetle into Liliane's face. She screamed and dropped the knife. Angela stepped on it so she couldn't retrieve it.

Emma grabbed Amin around his knees and pulled him to the floor as she stood. The drone hit him in the face, too, and his gun popped out of his hand as he tried to fight off the fake beetle. Chris scooped up the gun and pointed it toward Amin.

Now all he had to do was untie Angela's hands, but before Chris could move, the front door opened. He hoped it was Rick.

"Amin! Amin! You there?"

Amin screamed. "Shoot them! Shoot them now."

Two shots echoed in the small area, missing everyone, but sending books flying, several of which fell on Heinz.

Tex reached in the drawer where the drones had been and pulled out his pistol. Angela ducked. Chris shot the one on the right and Tex the one on the left. When the wounded men dropped out of sight, Chris wondered if they'd attack again.

Chris kept an eye out for the two men as he checked to see if everyone in the minibus was okay. Then he moved toward Angela. There was no time for more than a loving, relieved look and a quick kiss. He used Liliane's knife to cut the rope that held his wife's hands behind her back. He gave her Amin's gun and retrieved his own.

Chris nodded toward Amin. "Tex, keep an eye on him. Angela and I will check on the two who were shot."

Chris looked around before departing. Liliane shouldn't be a threat. She was still flicking her face to fight off imaginary beetles.

Angela took the front door and Chris the back. They silently coordinated their movement with their eyes and head nods as if they had partnered for years.

Sayid and Nizar lay on the ground outside the bookmobile, both face down with their hands tied behind their backs with plastic shackles.

Chris smiled when he saw who was responsible.

CHAPTER TWENTY-FOUR

Chris was relieved to see Nathan, Rick, and Jake had their weapons out as if daring the captured terrorists to make a move. Dr. Nolan was with them, but she was unarmed, probably there to fix wounds instead of cause them.

Rick spoke for the group. "We got a call from Michael in Texas. He said you might need some help."

"Thanks," Chris said. "We were getting ready to clean up the mess ourselves, but we welcome your assistance."

Rick holstered his pistol. "Looks like you've got everything under control. These two only have minor wounds. Dr. Nolan will look them over, but I don't think there's anything life threatening."

Nathan faced Angela. "You're covered with dried

blood. You okay, partner?"

"Alive." She looked down at her blouse. "I tried to keep one of the terrorists from bleeding to death. It didn't work. His body is in the van Amin and his mates pushed off the cliff. I'm tired, but not wounded."

"Good. We'll talk."

Angela stared at Nathan. "What happened to your eye?"

"Nothin'."

Chris locked glances with Nathan for a few seconds.

Jake held out a hand to Angela. "You must be Angela. I'm Jake. This is Rick and this is Polly."

Angela shook hands with each one. "Thanks for your help in the rescue. You sound like Americans. What's up?"

"We're FBI. Came here to find Emma. Looks like you've done that for us. We heard how you wouldn't leave without her, and we got the message you sent us via Chris, here. I assume she's inside."

Chris answered before Angela had a chance. "Yes. But, be careful with her. Angela can tell you more, but from what I witnessed, she acts more like an ISIS sympathizer than a kidnapped opera singer."

"Oh?" Rick asked. "Do you think they turned her?"

"I'm not sure. What do you think, Angela?"

Before Angela could answer, Liz lumbered out of the bookmobile and enveloped Angela in a bear hug. "I'm so glad you're safe."

After Liz hugged everyone, Nathan, Jake, and Polly went inside the minibus. Rick stayed to watch the shackled pair of terrorists.

Liz hugged Angela again and held on for what seemed like an eternity.

"Hey," Chris said, tugging Liz's arm, "it's my turn."

Liz let go of Angela and opened her arms toward Chris as if to hug him. She knew it was Angela he was talking about hugging, but Liz could see humor in any situation. He gave Liz a quick hug then took Angela into his arms and held her so long that when they separated, Liz and Rick were looking the other way, giving them more privacy.

Local police came over from the cliff-side rescue and exchanged IDs with Rick. They took custody of the two ISIS fighters.

Chris didn't like explaining guns to local police so he took his gun and Angela's and handed them to Tex who sat inside the minibus near the exit.

Chris took Angela's hand and led her to a spot near the end of the vehicle. When they were alone for the first time in what seemed like forever, he wrapped her in his arms and held her against him. "I missed you so much," he said. He kissed her.

Liz's voice boomed in his earpiece. "Hey! Did you know your mic is on?"

"Oops." Chris pulled the loop from under his shirt and briefly showed it to Angela. "Liz reminded me everyone can hear us.

Angela looked at him. "Are you wearing a comm?"

He touched his ear. "Of course. We're not bumpkins, you know. I forgot I had it on."

"The Vengeance Squad is getting high-tech." She

reached under his shirt and found the loop again. She spoke into it. "Thanks, Liz. We're signing off now." She flipped the power button off and let the device fall back into place on his chest.

"Oh, I guess I need to tell you about the conversation I had with Michael while we were transferring money for Amin."

"Michael? Liz's grandson? Is he here?"

"Only by comm. Physically he's in Texas. I'll tell you about it later. For now . . . " He pulled her in close again and hung on until he felt whole. He backed away and reached for her chin. He slowly turned her face toward his until their lips touched. Gently at first, then again and again. She responded at first, but not long enough. She squirmed out of his arms and pushed him away.

***

Angela inhaled, taking in the precious air to avoid passing out. She hadn't been caring for her body lately. She hadn't slept properly and hadn't eaten the appropriate foods. If that wasn't enough, she'd been on high alert, mentally as well as physically, for . . . she wasn't sure . . . for as long as she'd been held captive.

Chris pulled back to look into her eyes. "What's wrong?"

She saw his concern, but it couldn't be helped. He didn't know about the baby, and she hadn't verified what she knew with a test. She pulled him close and kissed him once, and again. "Nothing is wrong. I kinda lost my breath for a second." She smiled. "You do that to me, you know."

It didn't faze him. He had problems at times when words didn't match up with facts. His interpretation of facts. "You scared me," he said, ignoring what she said about kissing him taking her breath away.

"I know. I'm sorry."

He kissed her gently, "No need to apologize. It's your job."

"My job is to make you worry?" She laughed.

He cocked his head as if trying to determine what she thought was funny. "I mean your job as an agent for MI6. Yes, that makes me worry. More than I should, I know. I've always known something like this could happen. You told me not to worry, but you know that is impossible. Feelings just are. We can't control them. We can only hide them for a brief time if we have a reason to."

"I understand. And we both knew you wouldn't sit at home praying someone would do something to find me if this happened." She saw his eyes glistening from the beginning of tears. He didn't show his emotions often, so his tears were special. "Oh, Chris. I'm so sorry." She kissed his eyes, wanting to share his pain and lessen it some way.

He tried to wipe his face with his sleeve, but it didn't help much. "I love you too." He paused. "I guess I made it harder for you, knowing I was out there searching. But I couldn't help it. I had to find you. I don't think I could live without you." He turned his head.

She pulled him back and saw the tears rolling down his face. With her thumb, she wiped away each one and then hugged him again. "I'm not complaining. I'm not sure I could have made it this time without you doing what you did. And I'm sorry. For several reasons."

"What do you mean?" He had that cocked ear thing going stronger than before. It was time to tell him.

"I put your child in danger."

"My what?" His eyes popped open.

"You heard me. I'm pregnant." She hadn't done the test, but somehow, she knew she was right.

He cleared his voice. "Pregnant." It wasn't a question.

She nodded, smiling broader than before. "I didn't know until after I was kidnapped so I haven't verified it. But, I'm sure. We can get one of those home pregnancy tests until I can see the doctor."

"I'm going to be a father." This, also, wasn't a question.

She answered anyway. "Yes."

He pulled her close and held her. "A baby."

"Yes. I'm *pretty* sure."

He pushed away and looked at her sternly. "And, what are you going to do now?"

She wasn't sure what he was getting at. "Uh . . . I'm going to be a mother?"

"Yes, but first . . . ?"

"Uh . . . " She shrugged.

"You're going to request desk duty until the baby

is born."

She smiled. "Yes, dear. I promise not to put our baby in dangerous situations . . . again."

He kissed her. A kiss that lasted until Rick showed up.

"Oops, sorry," Rick said. "Didn't mean to interrupt your reunion."

Angela smiled. "That's okay. I wanted to thank you for showing up when you did. Those two terrorists would've attacked again if you hadn't been there to stop them."

"You can thank Chris for that. He tracked you to this place when no one else knew where you were and Michael told us you needed help."

Angela turned toward Chris and smiled. "He's good at that."

"We can debrief you later, but I have some questions about Emma and could use your input."

Angela was all business. "I'll help any way I can. I was with her every day since they nabbed me. I've lost track of how long that's been. I watched her change from an activist who passionately wanted to help the refugees to a scared little girl who slept most of the time, and then to a tough, take-charge type who stood up to the ISIS recruiter and his gang. She helped him near the end, but I think what she did was for survival. You'll need an expert to talk to her, but my opinion is that after some counseling, she'll be okay."

Rick nodded. "Good to know. We've got her parents in a hotel in Berlin. Maybe they can help."

"I'm sure they can," Angela said. "She's confused

right now, though. Her parents are divorced. She's called for her mother several times during the ordeal, but said she hasn't had a good relationship with her father.

"Keep a close watch on her. There's no telling what she might do. At the end of the confrontation she helped us by tripping Amin, but I don't know if she meant to help or was mad at him for slapping her when she said she wanted to be one of his generals."

"Wow. I see," Rick said. "Appreciate that." He turned to Chris. "We've got some locals coming to take custody of the ISIS team. Nathan set it up. You two okay with that? I'm not sure what the Germans will do with them. They may send them back to the refugee camps for all I know, but there's not much we can do about it. We have what we came for—Emma and Angela, right?"

Chris nodded. "It'd be a shame if the Germans don't lock them up. They should be tried for kidnapping and for Volker's murder. But, honestly, I only care about Angela." He turned to her. "How about you?"

Angela paused. "I didn't know about Volker's murder. I'm sorry to hear that. They're indirectly responsible for Burhan's death."

"Was Burhan the one in the van when it went over the cliff?" Rick asked.

Angela nodded. "Yes, he was one of the terrorists. He was shot at the Mitte Camp. This is off the record, I think both Chris and Tex shot him when they were trying to rescue me. Chris is an expert shot, and he never shoots to kill. Tex is a former marine taught to *always* shoot to kill."

Rick scratched his head. "I understand. We were here at the invitation of the government and they usually don't ask how we solve a case. However, if required, we'll have to help them with the investigations."

Angela nodded. "I understand. We must let the local government do what they're required to do. Even if it means the ISIS team goes free. If I ever see Amin or any of his gang in England, they'd better watch out."

The minibus door opened. Amin and Liliane came out first, both cuffed, followed by Jake. He ordered them to the ground next to their wounded friends. German police surrounded the prisoners.

Heinz helped Tex out of the bookmobile, both grinning. "We did it," Heinz said. "We caught the kidnappers and set their captives free. *Wunderbar!*"

Tex nodded. "It's a good feeling, isn't it? And to think, I almost stayed home this time."

Chris looked at him with one raised eyebrow. "You what?"

"Kidding. I've always got your back, Doc. You know that."

Angela kissed Tex on the cheek. "Thank you."

Liz and Emma came out next, Liz holding Emma's hand and helping her down the steps. When they were on solid ground, Liz hugged Emma and held her a little longer than Liz's longest hugs.

After Liz let her go, Emma backed up and faced Liz. "Mommy?"

Rick looked at Jake then gently cuffed Emma's hands behind her. "This is for your protection."

"Okay. Thank you." Emma's smile could melt an iceberg.

***

Angela felt Chris's arm hook in hers and she knew everything would be okay. She needed a hot bath, some clean clothes, and a proper English breakfast. But, the world was beginning to return to normal.

Being held by radical Islamic terrorists had been frightening because she never knew what they might do. She looked at Chris and squeezed her arm around his until he turned and looked back. They both smiled.

Chris turned to walk to the minibus, with Angela still holding on. He stopped at the door and turned to Rick. "Amin said he had a phone. One he could use to check on his bank balance after we transferred the money he demanded. I have the account number if you need it."

Rick smiled. "Good to know. Did you transfer money into his account?"

Chris paused, a simple grin on his face. "No. we transferred it *out*."

Tex laughed. "You did what?"

"We emptied his bank account."

Liz moved in closer, still holding an arm around Emma. "While he was looking over your shoulder?"

"Actually, it was Michael who did the transfer. I was too busy making Amin think I was stealing money for him. Remember when I read Amin's bank account out loud?"

"Yes," Tex said. "Yes. I wondered why you did that."

"Michael was listening and he took Amin's money out."

"Should I ask where you put the funds?" Rick asked.

"Don't worry," Chris said. "Michael put the money in a place where it can be used for good instead of evil. Liz will have to decide, but I'm thinking it should be used for the thousands of Germans who welcomed refugees into their country only to be harmed by the people they were trying to help."

Angela looked at Chris. She'd known he was a good man before she married him, but at times like this she was proud to be his wife. She stifled a laugh.

Heinz stepped closer. "As a German, I say 'thank you' for stopping these terrorists."

"Why me?" Liz asked. "We can all work together to find where the money should be used. Perhaps more counseling for victims or more security guards to prevent crimes. Repayment of ransoms paid to kidnappers."

"All of that sounds good," Chris said. "We can brainstorm it when we get home. I mentioned *you* simply because the money is in *your* bank account in Austin."

"Huh?" Liz's mouth fell open.

"It was the only bank account number Michael knew by heart."

Lis smiled. "Well, I'm honored. How much money are we talking about?"

"A little more than three million US dollars."

Tex slapped his leg in joy. "Wow. That's a bunch of dirty money. Or, it *was*. Now it can be used for good."

Rick smiled. "Okay, I'm not sure what to say about the money. Luckily, it's out of my jurisdiction. I gave your names to the local law enforcement. They'll contact us if they need statements or more information. You're all free to go. Emma, you'll need to come with us. Your parents are waiting for you in Berlin."

"Really?" Emma acted surprised. She looked at Liz for confirmation.

Liz nodded and hugged Emma again. "Yes, sweetie. Don't be afraid. Doctor Nolan and these men came all the way from America to find you. They will take you to your parents."

Angela gave Emma a hug, too. "Goodbye, Emma. I'm sure everything will be okay now. I want to go to one of your operas soon. I'll be watching for the announcement."

Emma looked at Angela. "Toi, toi, toi?"

Doctor Nolan took Emma's arm from Liz. "We'll watch over her and get her back on stage soon."

Jake looked around at the group. "We've got a helicopter waiting nearby to take us back to our plane. Anyone want a ride?"

Chris turned to Jake. "Thanks for the offer, but we've got to get the minibus back to Berlin and return it to our benefactors. Angela can ride with us. We still have hotel rooms there. So, we'll stay in the Mitte area tonight and go back to England tomorrow."

Rick nodded and shook each person's hand. "Okay. Be safe."

Jake said goodbye to everyone as well.

Nathan moved in front of Angela. "You need to be debriefed, you know."

She gave him her fiercest stare. "I know. But first I need a shower and a good meal. After that, some time with my husband. Debriefing will follow."

"But, it is required . . . "

Angela shook her head and wondered if she should tell him she was pregnant. She hadn't talked to Chris yet about who they would tell. "No, Nathan. I need time off. I'll answer your questions tomorrow. Besides, you know as much about this incident as I do. All the actors are in custody. Most everything has been wrapped up."

Nathan had his arms crossed. "I guess. Can you at least tell me what the ISIS gang was doing here? I mean here at the cliffs?"

"They were looking for a beach where they were supposed to meet a boat. From what I heard, I think they missed a turn along the way. When they saw the cliffs, they were turning around when the van gave out. I think the block got too hot from lack of oil. That's when they decided to get rid of the vehicle."

"And the body."

"Yes. The two guys you and Rick caught outside the bookmobile had been sent to steal another means of transportation. You may want to tell the locals. There's probably a car or truck missing and it can most likely be found around here somewhere." She indicated the surrounding area.

Nathan nodded. "I'll tell them. Thanks. And take as long as you want for that debriefing. We can do it next week if that's good for you. Yes, I agree you deserve some time off." He looked at Chris. "And he deserves some time to be with you. If it wasn't for his persistence, I'm not sure . . . ."

She smiled, knowing it was hard for Nathan to give Chris credit for finding and rescuing her. She leaned in and gave him a peck on the cheek. "I understand. Thanks, Nathan. See you next week."

She took Chris's arm in hers and they climbed into the minibus, leaving Nathan and the rest of the world outside. "Let's go home."

CHAPTER TWENTY-FIVE

When everyone was aboard, Chris turned to Heinz. "Can you drive this thing? I want to sit with Angela."

"Hey. I can drive." Liz was in the center of the bookmobile section with arms akimbo.

"I can, too." Tex removed his Stetson and tossed it on the table in the control center.

After all their years together, Chris still had trouble knowing when Tex was teasing. "You know this minibus is not set up for you to drive."

Tex laughed. "I *can* drive. Just not this particular vehicle."

"Well, it's set up for me." Liz pulled her wrinkled dress into place and dared Chris to disagree. "I drove a bookmobile bigger'n this in Texas."

"Yes, Liz," Chris said, "but, Heinz is German. It'll

be easier for him to take the wheel."

"Easier? Why?" Liz asked.

Chris wasn't sure why Liz cared. Was she making fun of him the way Tex did? Everyone liked to act up after a job was accomplished. Part of the relaxation process. And, yes, they even sometimes teased him because it took him so long to catch them at it.

"Liz, I know you'd be a perfect driver, but Heinz knows the German rules and can read the signs. I know most of the signs use symbols we all know, but from my experience behind the wheel in Germany, there are many signs I didn't understand."

"Ja. Be happy to drive." Heinz rubbed his hands together. "But only if I get hug from Miss Liz first."

Liz grinned and moved into his arms. "Oh, you . . . " She seemed to forget all about driving.

Chris handed Heinz the keys. "Angela, you've met Heinz Gabriel, right?"

Heinz looked sheepishly at her.

She smiled. "I know Heinz. We've worked together several times. How'd you get him in the Vengeance Squad?"

Chris smoothed his mustache toward his chin. He sure needed a trim. "Nathan sent him to spy on us. When we found out, we stole him from Nathan. I'm sure you'll hear about that later. Nathan wasn't so happy about it."

"Ja," Heinz said. "I will probably never work for you again, Miss Angela."

"We'll see about that," she said. "Nathan tends to make unfortunate decisions from time to time. I can get you reinstated."

Heinz smiled. "Thank you."

"Okay," Chris said, "is everyone ready to go back to the hotel in Mitte? We'll get cleaned up and go out somewhere fancy for dinner. It'll be a celebration. Then tomorrow, we'll return the vehicle to our benefactors and take the train home." He motioned toward Angela. "Our home, that is. The rest of you will have a ways to go, but you're welcome to stay in Bath as long as you like."

Chris and Angela took seats in the back of the minibus. He leaned over to whisper. "Okay, if I tell them about 'you know what'?"

She put her lips to his ear. "Let's wait until I have verification. How about tomorrow night in Bath?"

He shivered from her nearness and didn't trust his voice. He nodded.

***

Angela was surprised to see her suitcase when she and Chris got to the hotel room. "You found my things. I'm impressed."

Chris nodded. "Yes, of course. There's more."

He opened the room safe and extracted her purse along with her bra with the RFID chip and her GPS watch. "Who's Charlene Frank?"

She knew he would have determined that it was her MI6 alias. "Don't ask. And don't be surprised if the name gets archived."

She opened the suitcase and pulled out a set of

clean clothes. "Thanks for getting my clothes for me. I don't know what I thought I would wear tonight after my shower."

Chris looked at her a few seconds as if deciding how much he should say. Finally, he said it. "I may have given Nathan that black eye."

She looked at him with raised eyebrows, forcing him to say more.

"We'd tracked your RFID chip and were about to go in the building to rescue you. Instead, Nathan came out and said you weren't there. Our RFID reader said he had the chip. We took it and I may have hit him a bit hard for not telling us what he'd found."

"That's okay. He should have shared the information with you."

"Yes, but . . . in hindsight, he may have been trying to protect me from showing your . . . clothes in front of everyone."

She laughed. "I doubt he'd think that way. Don't worry about it. He deserved that shiner."

She wasn't as hungry as she thought she'd be. But, apparently everyone else was. Instead of going out somewhere fancy to celebrate, they ended up in the hotel restaurant, mainly because it was the nearest place. The food was good and everyone ordered dinners with lots of bread, salad, and sides.

Angela didn't see anything on the menu that interested her so she'd ordered soup and salad. The salad alone was too big for one person to consume, but she felt better eating something other than bologna sandwiches that consisted of bread and occasionally meat. She didn't think she would ever eat another sandwich.

Chris was the only one who cleaned his plate. He devoured his veal and *spätzle* in a matter of minutes. He waited politely while she worked on her soup and salad.

After dinner, they made plans to meet for breakfast and all said goodnight.

As Angela and Chris got ready for bed, she worried what he might have in mind. "You know that old headache excuse?"

"Uh . . . yes." He cocked his head to listen.

"Tonight, I have a *real* headache."

His expression didn't change, but she knew he understood. "But I could sure use a hug."

He raised an eyebrow. "Should I call Liz?"

***

Chris watched with pleasure as Angela devoured her proper English breakfast, German style. After seeing her pick at her food the night before, he was glad she was eating more this morning. After all, she had to eat enough for two now.

Afterward they packed up and met outside the hotel for one last ride in the minibus. Chris had talked to the benefactors and they had hired Heinz to take the minibus to Darmstadt where it was to be refitted as a bookmobile and donated to the library there. He would first drop the rest of the team at the train station for the trip to Bath.

Rick and Jake arrived before they climbed aboard the minibus. "Anyone need a ride?" Rick asked.

"No," Chris said. "Heinz is taking us to the train station."

"I don't mean a ride to the train. I'm talking about a ride to the States. When I told headquarters how much you all had helped us rescue Emma, they told me to fly you back to Texas."

Tex twisted his wheelchair around to face Rick. "Texas? Free flight? Shucks, yeah, I want a ride home."

"Good. How about you, Liz?"

"Thanks for the offer, but I can't. My husband is waiting for me at Angela's house in Bath."

Rick scratched his head. "Bath? Hmm. I think we could stop there on the way. I'll have to check with the pilot. If we can, do you want to go with us?"

Liz didn't hesitate. "Yes, of course."

Rick pulled out his phone and made a call. When he disconnected, he smiled. "Can do. We'll fly you all to Bath, drop off Chris and Angela, pick up Liz's husband and fly you to Austin, Texas. How does that sound? I think the government owes you that much for rescuing Emma."

Chris looked at Angela. "Uh . . . can you take time for everyone to come to our house in Hemington for dinner? We'd like to have a farewell party. We don't get to see each other often."

Angela nodded. "Yes. We have something we want to share with everyone."

"That's nice," Liz said.

"Hope it's another one of those lamb shanks," Tex said.

Chris looked at Rick. "You're all invited, too."

Rick turned to Jake who nodded. "We can't speak for Polly, but I suspect she'll be in favor of it. We could use a little time off."

They all said goodbye to Heinz and climbed into Rick's van for the trip to the airport.

***

It was Angela's first look at the FBI plane and she wished MI6 provided transportation like that for her. But, then she remembered she was going on maternity leave anyway so it didn't matter.

They landed at Bristol Airport and took the Black Chevy Suburban to Hemington, twenty miles away. Jake and Rick went with them. Polly decided to stay in Bristol to meet up with an old friend she hadn't seen in years.

As they neared the farmhouse, Liz pointed. "There's Samuel, waiting outside. Isn't he sweet?"

"Who is that woman standing next to him?" Angela asked, giving Chris a knowing wink.

Liz stretched her neck trying to get a better look. "Why . . . that's . . . " She guffawed. "I can't believe it. That's Jane!"

Tex's head had been bobbing as he'd napped during the drive from the airport, but the mention of his wife's name woke him. He pushed his hat high on his head and strained to see out the front window.

"What? Jane's here? How'd that happen? I talked to her last night and she didn't say a word about coming to meet me." He scratched his head. "Oh my gosh, she must've been here when I talked to her and wanted to surprise me." His grin covered his face and his eyes glistened. "I sure missed her."

As they neared Samuel and Jane, Michael stepped out from behind them. Liz teared up and couldn't speak. She tried to, but nothing came out. Instead she pointed and continued to cry.

"Michael helped us with this adventure so much," Chris said, "I thought it only right that he get to ride back with you and Samuel."

Liz gave Chris a kiss on the cheek. "Thank you." Her voice was husky, but it finally worked.

Chris explained. "You can thank Brian and Angela. When he heard we'd finished the job, he asked if there was anything we needed. Angela suggested sending Jane and Michael over. This was before we learned about the FBI plane ride offer."

Liz hugged Angela. "Thank you, dear. With all you've been through, you still took time to think of others. Michael didn't have a passport. How did he get one so quickly?"

"With our help," Jake answered. "The FBI fast-tracked it for him. By the way, who is this Brian you mentioned?"

"One of our benefactors," Chris said. "Brian Donelson and his Combine friends like to support good causes. He paid our expenses for this trip and provided the minibus and all the equipment. He made the rescue possible. Liz, maybe we should offer to repay the Combine with some of Amin's money."

She nodded. "Good idea. They can surely find a way to use the money for other worthy projects."

"Brian sounds like a fine man to know," Rick said as he parked in front of the farmhouse.

Tex banged his fist on his wheelchair arm. "Let me outta here. I need to hug my wife."

"Hold your horses," Liz said. "Don't worry, I'll hug her while the guys get you out."

"You get to hug everybody," Tex said.

Liz bent over and hugged Tex on her way to the door.

Angela followed Liz out and Chris helped Rick and Jake lift Tex and his wheelchair and set it on the pavement.

Liz quickly hugged Jane. "Good to see you. There's a mighty happy man clamoring to get to you. What a wonderful surprise."

Liz gave Samuel a huge smile, but he pushed Michael toward her so she hugged him first. The tears returned.

Michael looked into her eyes. "You okay, GiGi?"

She pulled him tight. "Yes. I'm happy to see you, that's all." She seemed to be having trouble talking again. "Most of all, I'm proud of you."

Chris shook Michael's hand. "We're all proud of you. We couldn't have done it without you. Thank you."

Liz took her time hugging Samuel. "Miss me?"

"Did I ever!" He said it like he meant it. In his usual way, he hugged her back.

Angela got to him next. "Uncle Samuel, I'm sorry I caused all this trouble."

Samuel teared up. "Don't worry yourself about that. We're happy you're home safe."

Angela gave him a peck on the cheek. "Did you have any problems finding the groceries Chris asked for?"

"Not at all. The lamb shank is done. I followed Chris's instructions and set it off the charcoal to stay warm. It looks and smells delightful. Jane helped with the trimmings. We're ready to eat anytime you are."

Angela kissed her uncle again. "Good."

She watched as Tex rolled over to Jane. They looked at each other with misty eyes like a couple of teenagers getting back together after being away from each other for the summer. Angela could tell words weren't needed for those two. They must have reached a point in their marriage where being in the same locale was enough to spark pure happiness. Angela felt that way about Chris, too.

Jane helped Tex into the house. There were no ramps, and plenty of rocks, but they managed.

Angela and Chris met Rick and Jake at the door. "Welcome to the farm," she said.

Rick took a deep breath. "Something smells good."

Chris showed them into the house. "Samuel has a lamb shank ready. We'll eat in a few minutes."

Angela paused. "Before we do, I wanted to ask about Emma. How is she doing?"

Jake shook his head. "Not so good. We thought getting her with her parents would help her recover. But it hasn't."

"Not yet anyway," Rick said. "She's ignored her mother and dad and asked about you and Liz."

"With her parents' approval, we're keeping her in custody for her own safety. She's at Ramstein Air Force Base in Germany where she can get the medical treatment she needs. They're better suited to take care of her there than we are. Her parents went with her."

Chris ran a hand through his hair. "Ramstein? Isn't that where the military sends wounded service members?"

"That's right. They have all the latest medical facilities there," Jake said.

"I hope she recovers," Angela said. "She had a budding opera career which means she has special talents."

Rick nodded. "My experience in cases like this is that we can expect a full recovery."

"That's good to hear," Chris said.

"You'll let us know?" Angela said. "We'll be praying for her. And feel free to call on me if you think it would help to visit her. We spent a lot of time together."

"Thanks. I'll tell the docs at Ramstein about your offer and keep you posted."

Chris led the way. "Okay, let's eat."

***

After dinner, during dessert and coffee, Chris tapped a knife on his glass to get everyone's attention. "Angela has an announcement."

She looked at him with eyebrows arched. "I think he means *he* has something he'd like to say."

He smiled and held out opened arms as if pleading with her.

She stood. "But, I'll do it for him . . . for us."

She looked around the room. "We'd like to thank everyone for helping to free me. In my work, I sometimes forget the impact my job makes on the family back home. This time, it came to me clearly what each of you did for me."

She made eye contact with each person at the table. "For example, Tex had to leave a busy counseling practice, one that took years to grow. Jane had to take vacation from work to be here today and before that she had to take care of their children without Tex's help. Michael helped us from Texas while caring for the farm and keeping the bookmobile service available. Thank you all."

She locked eyes with Liz and paused. "I'm especially thankful for you. You're the stabilizing force for this group. If you hadn't been there, Tex and Chris would have tried to solve every problem with a gun and computer. You don't put up with guns, and computers will always be a mystery to you."

Liz laughed. "That's for sure. But, they're such good boys."

Angela continued. "Thank you, Uncle Samuel, for taking care of the house and for lending me your wife."

He nodded. "Anytime, my dear. But, I hope there won't be another time like this one where we didn't know where you were."

"And, finally, thank you, Jake and Rick, and the rest of your team back at the plane. We appreciate your special contributions."

Angela sat. The room was suddenly quiet.

Chris looked around. "And . . . ?"

Angela pretended not to know what he meant.

He stood. "You know, the rest. The news. The announcement."

"Announcement? I thanked everyone."

"But, what about the *baby*?" He couldn't help himself.

Liz was on her feet. "Baby? Are you two having a baby?"

Angela had hardly nodded her head when she was grabbed by Liz for one of her famous hugs. This time, they ended up dancing around the room.

When all were somewhat calmed, Jane hugged Angela, too. "What about your work?"

Chris wrapped an arm around Angela. "She's taking a little time off because of the nature of the recent assignment."

Tex rolled up to them. "If you have some time off, why don't you visit us in Texas?"

Chris and Angela looked at each other. "We decided to go see my parents in California . . . "

Tex's lip turned down. "Aw . . . well . . . I understand. Kinda wanted to show you my new office and all. And the kids . . . they sure miss you, you know."

Chris continued. "But, we could stop by on the way to California."

Tex beamed.

"Come to Georgetown, too," Liz said. "You haven't seen our farm, yet."

Angela nodded. "We will. You don't think we'd get that close to Georgetown and not visit, do you?"

"There's more news," Angela said. "MI6 has offered Chris a contract to improve security on their computers. They feel that since he could break in perhaps he can tell them why and help make their computer systems more secure. And that means more work for Michael, too."

Michael looked at Chris and they both smiled.

Rick put an arm on Chris's shoulder. "I hope you'll still have time to work with the FBI."

"Don't worry, the FBI will continue to be my primary job—that plus finishing my novel about the computer nerd who marries a spy."

"Uh-oh." Liz was looking at her phone. "I got a message from the Georgetown Police Department. There's been another murder and they want me to help investigate."

ACKNOWLEDGEMENTS

I think much of the success of my previous novel, *Murder in Sun City*, was due to the comments and suggestions from my critique team. That's why I worked with the same friends while writing this book.

D.A. Featherling and C. Wayne Dawson, the other two members of the team, helped me in many ways. A major reason to work with a critique team is to force yourself to write on a regular basis. Left on my own, I might go for days, even weeks, without writing a word and find dozens of ways to justify the lack of productivity. Peer pressure is hard to ignore. We began with a goal of 1,500 words a week and later upped it to 2,000. Sometimes what I submitted was short of the goal and not my best work, but the total word count grew with my effort to not disappoint my friends. I'm not sure they experienced the same problems I did. D.A. Featherling wrote two books while I struggled to finish mine. C. Wayne Dawson finished his third historical novel, one that required many hours of research.

We edited by email mostly and met monthly to discuss each other's work. We limited the discussion to fifteen minutes per person per book. For me the corrections and suggestions received resulted in changes in story direction as well as character development. In addition, I learned to be a better editor by reading and commenting on their work.

Advance readers for this book were Malia Barth, Anne Frohlich, Celeste Frost, Shirley Nash, Lois Stanley, and Chuck Zook. I gave the advance readers an earlier version of the book this time. As a result, they provided more than proofreading. They also told me what worked and what didn't. A special thanks to all of you. This book wouldn't be the same without your input.

I would also like to thank my editor, Lisa Lickel. She did an excellent job correcting my mistakes and pointing out where more (or less) was needed. She didn't often make changes in the text, but she did insert questions to trigger me to do so.

I used two proofreaders this time and didn't let them start work until I felt the manuscript was perfect. I dared them to find anything wrong. And, of course they did. D.A. Featherling is a writer who is familiar with my work and Malia Barth is a reader who finds mistakes faster than most people read.

Even with all this help, errors will creep in. They always do. However, with today's technology, we can quickly clean them out. I'm counting on you, the reader, to find the rest of the errors. Let me know if you find anything that doesn't sound right. And if you do, don't be surprised if I ask you to be an advance reader for the next book.

As you read in the last paragraph of this book, the next one will be another Liz Helmsley mystery set in Georgetown, Texas. That is unless the Vengeance Squad gets activated first.

Sidney W. Frost
June 5, 2017
Georgetown, Texas

ABOUT THE AUTHOR

Sidney W. Frost grew up in Austin, Texas, served in the US Marines in California, worked in the space industry in Los Angeles and Houston, and lives in Georgetown, Texas.

He has loved choral music from an early age, and was in 42 Austin Opera productions. He and his wife, Celeste, sing in their church choir as well as a community chorus that performs with the symphony in Georgetown and Temple, Texas. They have also participated in several Berkshire Festivals in and out of the United States. He loves to travel and has visited 33 countries.

He has a Master of Science degree from the University of Houston and a Bachelor of Arts from the University of California at Long Beach. He has worked in the Information Technology business for many years, and in May 2011, retired after thirty years as an Adjunct Professor of Computer Science at Austin Community College. He received the adjunct teaching excellence award in 2005. He still enjoys teaching and is available for workshops and seminars. His most recent class was one on memoir writing for the Senior University of Georgetown.

He is the author of six novels, set in and around Austin, Texas. Awards for his novels include First Place in the 2007 SouthWest Writers Contest and First Place in the 2007 Writers' League of Texas Novel Manuscript Contest.

He has more than 140,000 readers in 15 countries!

AFTERWORD

Thank you for reading *The Vengeance Squad Goes to Germany*. If you haven't already, I hope you will read *Where Love Once Lived, Love Lives On, The Vengeance Squad, The Vengeance Squad Goes to England,* and *Murder in Sun City*. See my website, http://sidneywfrost.com, for the latest information about all my books.

If you would like to see images for this book, go to:
https://www.pinterest.com/sidneywfrost/the-vengeance-squad-goes-to-germany/

You may also want to visit my blog:
http://christianbookmobile.blogspot.com/

This is where I talk about writing, review books, interview other Christian authors and occasionally talk about growing up in Austin, Texas.

I also respond to email queries and would love to

hear from you: sidfrost@suddenlink.net.

I am also available to speak to your church or other group. Here is a list of classes I've taught or can teach:

- Basic Creative Writing
- Novel Writing
- Memoir Writing
- Converting Memoirs to Novels
- Self-Publishing vs. Traditional Publishing
- Creating E-Books
- Book Marketing

The length of each class can be adjusted to your schedule.

www.ingramcontent.com/pod-product-compliance
Lightning Source LLC
Chambersburg PA
CBHW060853250626
47159CB00008B/2714